A Last Glass of Tea
and Other Stories

A LAST GLASS OF TEA
and Other Stories

Mohamed El-Bisatie

Translated by
Denys Johnson-Davies

A THREE CONTINENTS BOOK
LYNNE RIENNER PUBLISHERS
BOULDER & LONDON

Published in the United States of America in 1998 by
Lynne Rienner Publishers, Inc.
1800 30th Street, Boulder, Colorado 80301

English-language translation © 1994, 1998 by Denys Johnson-Davies. All rights reserved by the publisher

Arabic text © 1970, 1979, 1988, 1992, 1993 by Mohamed El-Bisatie

Library of Congress Cataloging-in-Publication Data
Bisāṭī, Muḥammad.
   [Short stories. English. Selections]
   A last glass of tea and other stories / Mohamed El-Bisatie ;
translated by Denys Johnson-Davies. — 1st U.S. ed.
   p. cm.
   ISBN 0-89410-800-X (alk. paper)
   I. Johnson-Davies, Denys. II. Title.
PJ7816.I762 1998
892'.736—dc20   95-22229
                                                                     CIP

Printed and bound in the United States of America

∞   The paper used in this publication meets the requirements of the American National Standard for Permanence of Paper for Printed Library Materials Z39.48-1984.

5 4 3 2 1

Contents

Translator's Introduction	vii
The Wastelands	3
At the Roadside	7
Wild Mulberries	14
My Grandfather	16
A Last Glass of Tea	25
On the Brink	35
The Hill	41
Drought	44
A Weak Light Revealing Nothing	47
The Bend of the River	55
The Girl Washes	58
Death Has Its Time	61
The Floating Sack	69
A Conversation at Night	76
The Prisoner	83

Contents

The Condemned Man	87
A Conversation from the Third Floor	90
Confrontation	96
Uncle Zeydan	103
That's How It Was	112
The Trap	116
Meeting	120
Hagg Abd Rabbuh	124
War Widows	134
Sources	139
About the Author	141

Translator's Introduction

Denys Johnson-Davies

Ever since Mahmoud Teymour pioneered the short story in the 1930s and 1940s, Egypt has produced a number of writers who have practiced the genre with distinction, most recently Yahya Taher Abdullah, Yusuf Idris, and Yahya Hakki. Of those alive today there remain but few writers of real talent exercising this favored form of writing in the Arab world, and of these few, one whose work demands to be made known in the West is Mohamed El-Bisatie.

He was born in the Nile Delta in a small town overlooking the large salt lake of Manzala, and it is this area that he has made the canvas for almost all his writings, which include six volumes of short stories, the first published in 1968, and four novellas. His adult life has been lived in Cairo, except for a spell of five years in Saudi Arabia. Though in the intervening years he has felt no need to renew his acquaintance with his birthplace, it continues to be vividly etched in his imagination and remains the venue for these stories.

Highly regarded by critics and fellow writers in Cairo, El-Bisatie is a "writer's writer"—which is to say a writer who makes no concessions to the lazy reader. El-Bisatie stands back from his canvas and sketches his characters and events with a studied detachment. While there is drama in his stories it is never highlighted: the menace

Translator's Introduction

lurks almost unseen between the lines. The characters depicted in his stories are for the most part peasants and farmers or petty officials and shopkeepers; the general atmosphere is one of sparseness, and the ever-present dryness of the surroundings is echoed in the life of the protagonists. There is only the occasional passing reference to some historical event—such as Nasser's revolution in "A Weak Light Revealing Nothing" or Sadat's journey to Israel in "A Conversation at Night"—to indicate the time in which the stories are set. Historical events are not a part of the narratives; they occur off-stage and do not impinge on the lives of these villagers. The cold camera lens that is trained on the life events of these stories is equally matter-of-fact where death has a part, as for instance in the stark, steady tread of "Drought," and in the detachment of "The Hill," where the fate of the woman is merely a part of nature's intrusion, no more dramatic than the way in which the sea forms rock pools. The story "Death Has Its Time," with its extension "The Floating Sack," begins with the bald statement that the inhabitants of the lane know that a girl will be murdered that night. The effect of the story is in no way diminished by this knowledge of the ending at the start.

El-Bisatie writes with unrivaled authenticity of village life in a particular area of Egypt. Most important, though, he writes stories that are universal in their appeal.

A Last Glass of Tea
and Other Stories

The Wastelands

Our village looks over the lake. We are separated from it by vast tracts of wasteland covered by a fine layer of brittle salt, cane reeds that quickly wither, and thorn bushes that get tangled up into vast balls that are plucked up by the winds and thrown about ceaselessly until they end up in tatters in the streets of the village.

The wastelands have remained desolate throughout the years. When we were young we would run over there in our venturing to discover unknown lands. We would not go far away: all too soon we would be scorched by the blazing sun and the salt-filled wind. And today too we see the boys exploring over there.

Sometimes the gypsies come at the seasons of their migration. They set up their tents somewhere in the middle of the wastelands. After spending as long as they want there they then go off, unseen by anyone.

The buildings of our village were spreading out in the other direction, in the direction of the river.

❖

The people of our village don't care for fishing: they've never shown any enthusiasm for it. They had their trades which had been passed down to them and which, though they provided little profit, were sufficient for them.

The fishermen would come to our lake from the neighboring villages. We would see them in the middle of the night, the fishing nets on their backs covered over with canvas. They would stop at the shops to buy matches and tobacco.

The Wastelands

They would not show themselves to be in any hurry. They would turn their faces away from the bright light of the pressure-lamp and would sometimes sit beside the café that was still open and which looked onto the bridge, before crossing it into the darkness of the wastelands—drinking glasses of tea, then going off.

The villagers would await their return in the morning at the bridge, buying from the catch they had brought, and the fishermen would wash in the waters of the river, wash their baskets and nets, and depart.

Eventually they set up small huts of reed canes on the shore. They would leave their things there until they returned. When there was a run of fish their women and children would follow them, and they would spend days over there continuously fishing, with their women carrying the catch to the village, where the merchants would be waiting on the bridge.

They also used to get into fights. Those last hours when the run of fish began to wear off—we too awaited that time with great wariness. All too soon news of the fighting would reach us: fishermen from one neighboring village with fishermen from another. We would see one of them winding a rag round his injured head as he came from the wastelands and rushed to the station to leave the village. Then we would see them—the strangers—descending from the train and moving to the village like a small dark cloud. Among them were women dressed in black, and men holding sticks, and a man in a clean gallabia with a white shawl round his neck who walked in front of them and hired the horse carriage and the two donkey carts, while the others stood to one side, looking around at one another as they waited for him. Then they would go off with their carts to the wastelands.

We would see them when they returned, generally at the beginning of the night. The man with the white shawl—riding in the horse carriage with the women—and behind him a donkey cart strewn with wet grasses where the

The Wastelands

wounded, covered over with the black outer garments of the women, would be stretched out. We would walk alongside the cart, staring into the eyes of the wounded. We would, however, soon beat a retreat on hearing the angry remonstrations issuing from the last carriage. Then we would see them—the families of the wounded from the other village—getting down from the train and hiring carts and going off to the wastelands.

Sometimes the two groups would come at the same time, and it would seem as though each were avoiding the other. One of them would take its time in walking so that the other could hire its carts and go off, each one taking a track amid the wastelands. They never engaged in battle while they were transporting their wounded. We would wait at the bridge until they all returned from the lake, then we would go off to our homes. During those days it was dangerous to go near the wastelands, as each of the two groups would be lying in wait for the other. We wouldn't see them when they came or went, but we were always aware of them over there. Somehow or other they would have crept in and would be hiding in the hollows or among the reeds.

No one of us has anything to do with fishing. The men and the women, all dressed in black, still come from one day to another. They hire carts and go off to the wastelands, then return with their wounded. The others come after them.

Generally we leave our houses when the sun's heat abates. We walk about and pay visits and do our shopping. We stop for a while at the bridge, where we gaze at the wastelands, those vast tracts over which reign silence and stillness, the horizon aglow with the light of sunset.

❖

Once again the fish are in abundance along the shoreline and a coldish wind blows onto the village. Green grass has begun to sprout, scattered over the verges of the wastelands. Spatterings of rain catch up with the dust storms that gather in their path to the village.

The Wastelands

We see the fishermen walking once again with their nets. They seem to have stopped their quarreling. Crouched alongside the café, they are drinking tea and looking at us with sleepy eyes. When one of them finishes his glass of tea, he places it by the wall, takes up his net and goes off. Always they are silent. And when they are walking along the road on their way to the wastelands they look as though they see no one.

All too soon the fighting between them would break out and once again our doors would be closed after the evening prayer. Sometimes the fighting would advance right up to within the boundaries of the village. We would hear the sound of intermittent rifle fire drawing nearer, then the shots would be echoing right in front of the houses. Each time it would appear that this was their decisive battle. There were screaming women in the streets, hurrying feet, stifled cries, and the sound of sticks exchanging blows under the windows, then silence would reign. We would hear the sound of carts being dragged from behind the houses.

In the morning it would look as if nothing had happened. We would see the café in the market with its windows smashed, and the broken chairs in the square, and bits of sticks and drops of blood that hadn't dried.

And the boys would be happily searching around for empty cartridges.

At the Roadside

The shack stood at the entrance to the village alongside the road that led to the settlements. It had always been there, ever since we were boys climbing the trees around it. Those coming from the settlements would sit in its shade drinking tea and resting their tired feet before entering the village. And before setting off on their journey back to the settlements, they would stay there for a while as they searched around for some animal to ride or for some companion with whom to chat on the way.

Its owner was a skinny old man who would come early in the morning, making his way through the fields, followed by one of his grandsons, who would spread a mat on the stone bench in front of the shack, sprinkle some water around it, and wash the cups and the teapot in the canal. The old man kept a single sound wooden chair, which he would bring to the outside of the shack whenever some well-bred person arrived. If it was a woman, she would invariably disappear from sight behind the shack, wrapped in her black garment as she waited for a horse-carriage going in the direction of the settlements.

Beside the shack were some palm trunks thrown down by the side of the road. On market days the old man would spread sacks over them.

At night he would light a fire and sit beside it, fighting off sleep.

After evening prayers the village men would come. They liked to walk along the dirt road after a substantial supper, and would discharge their ringing laughs and ribald jokes

At the Roadside

into the darkness. Finally they would gather around the shack, spread out on the palm trunks. The old man would make tea as he listened to their noisy conversation. He would laugh silently and shake his head.

It was after the evening prayers, too, that the patrolmen would come. They did not have a fixed time and the week might pass without them coming anywhere near the village, then they would put in an appearance on two consecutive nights. They would enter the village by the weighbridge road where, after sunset, there were few travelers, and they would walk alongside the canal, then make a stop at the shack, when the old man would get to his feet, drying his eyes that were watering from the smoke. Silence would reign, and the men who had been leaping about on the track would go back to the palm trunks. They would cough breathlessly and begin to dry their sweat. They had heard much about the rough way the patrol officer treated even the important men. He would stand in front of the fire, his round white face taking on the colors reflected from the flames, staring into them with his sleepy eyes and licking the ends of his mustache. That habit of his, too, they had heard about. Behind him could be seen the heads of the horses as they grazed on the grasses at the roadside. The men would get up and brush the dust from their white gallabias. From the long yawns they gave it would be apparent that they were feeling tired and wanted to go to sleep, and they'd walk off arm in arm to the village.

The old man would carry the chair to the back of the shack and give a prod to his grandson sleeping inside. He would drag the woolen wrap off him and spread it on the stone bench. He would tie up the horses and bring them water from the canal, then seat himself by the fire to make tea. The soldiers paid nothing: they would drink as much tea as they liked and go off in peace. They would relax on the stone bench and he would bring them the water-pipe, laughing and saying, as he pressed down with his finger on the small live coals, "You've got a long journey."

At the Roadside

He took a glass of tea to the officer behind the shack, and the officer motioned him away. The old man said, "The glass is clean."

The officer again motioned to him to move away. He stood beside the chair with his hands behind his back, the stick covered with thin strips of leather under his arm. Each time he came he would stand in the same place, staring toward the fields that stretched away and the lights of the settlements that seemed from afar to be scattered in an uneven arc. From here things seemed clear: it could only be them. From its lights, the fishermen's settlement looks to be the nearest one to the district administration office, with only the lake between them. And yet when he went there with his horsemen it would prove to be the furthest away. How easily they could get to the district office and back in their boats! Who could catch them on the lake? Had the commissioner of police granted his request to set up a control center behind the district office and provide it with a force of several armed boats, the matter would have been resolved. The commissioner had shouted, "Launches with machine guns? Shall I tell them we can't catch a few cattle-thieves?"

Each time he would say that this time they wouldn't get away, and always they would choose the right time, just when the bales of cotton were waiting for the carts and the baskets of peaches were all stacked up near the gate of the Inspectorate, the maize and the wheat too.

Perhaps they hide the animals on the islands that are scattered throughout the lake. Or perhaps they handed them over immediately to one of the merchants. But those sacks that they fill with oranges and guavas, how is it he finds no trace of them at the settlement? He searches the houses one by one, the flat roofs and the baking ovens. He follows them directly after the raid, telling himself they wouldn't have time to hide what they have stolen. If only he had some boats he would catch them on the lake. However, each time he would ride along the dirt roads, passing by villages and

At the Roadside

settlements, in a hopelessly wide detour, there being no other road suitable for the horses.

Sometimes he would go after them two or three days after the raid, thinking they may have relaxed and removed their spoils or brought them from the islands. Each time he would sense that they were waiting for him. The settlement would appear to be empty, the houses shut and the lights turned off—even the shop that was like a crevice in the wall. He would sense their presence behind the doors watching him, and he would tremble with rage and strike at the doors with his foot. Those silently dumb faces. No one. That's how it was: the men were away fishing on the lake. Always fishing. No one but some old people on the heaps of straw in the houses, staring at him and getting to their feet.

"How do you know they're from the fishermen's settlement?" the superintendent would ask.

If only he had come and stood here and looked at those lights.

He walks for a while behind the shack, striking with his stick at the tips of the crop at the edge of the field.

"Ah, they rob the Inspectorate!"

He listens to the coughing of the soldiers on the stone bench and their whispered conversation with the old man, as though exhausted by the long silence as they followed him.

When he felt the horses had rested, he appeared suddenly in front of the shack and made his way to his horse, and they set off for the settlements.

The old man stood beside the blazing fire listening to the thud of the horses' hooves and turned round and called out to his grandson crouching at the door of the shack. "Go to Hagg Fathi. Tell him they're coming."

The boy spun round and rushed off through the fields in the direction of the fishermen's settlement. There was no clearly defined way through the fields, though the people in the settlements, when in a hurry, found a way to the village between the plots of land and the canals. The

At the Roadside

boy would go and come back before the patrol arrived at the settlement.

The old man gathered up his things and took them into the shack. He then closed the door and sat beside the fire, feeding it pieces of dry wood. He dozed off, giving himself up to the warmth and the silence. He was conscious of the rustle of vegetation behind the shack and whispered, as a slight tremor passed through his closed eyes, "Are you back?"

The boy nodded in silence and lit the kerosene lamp. The two of them wrapped themselves round in their cloaks and departed.

The patrol returned at a late hour. The horses were breathing heavily, slowing down as they neared the shack, and the soldiers glanced about them, hoping that the old man was still there. The officer himself said nothing when they asked him to rest the horses.

They would say to the old man, "Can't you wait a little till we return?" And the old man would say with a laugh, "I've been waiting and my bones are dried up from the cold—God help you." Many of the men of the village knew the secret, and each time the patrol arrived they would disperse far from the shack, exchanging glances in the darkness and murmuring among themselves, "It's a good thing the old man's doing—let him run about on his horse and lick his mustache."

After that they found another officer coming with the patrol and they discussed at length what had happened to the previous one at the fishermen's settlement when he began striking at the women with his leather-covered stick.

The women had shouted and screamed. They had then hurled bricks at him from the flat roofs. He, too, had been shouting and screaming as he pranced about on his horse in the alleys. Then, suddenly, he had darted off toward the lake. He charged back and forth along the shore, giving the reins to his mount. The soldiers had stood to one side, unable to

At the Roadside

keep up with him, then, not wanting anyone to see what was happening, they began to strike out at the villagers and drive them away from the shore. Then they heard the fearful shout he gave and they saw him drawing his revolver and firing shots in the direction of the lake.

"He's gone crazy," said Mukhtar the barber—and he walked slowly out of his shop and spat. Then, with a gesture of despair, he went back in.

"He shoots bullets at the water," said the men of the village. "Is it reasonable? Aren't bullets, too, to be accounted for?"

The patrolmen, who clearly didn't want to talk about these matters, said simply that he no longer went out with the patrol. Later they said they had seen shapes of people on the surface of the lake when the officer had fired the shots. The villagers listened to them and murmured, "Yes, of course."

Nothing changes in our village: we do just as our forefathers used to do. The old man carried the chair for the new officer to the back of the shack. We saw him standing beside it staring out at the lights of the distant settlements. He asked him the first time he brought him the glass of tea, "Is that...?" and he pointed the end of his leather-covered stick toward the lake, "Is that the fishermen's settlement?"

"It is, sir." At which the officer motioned him away.

The old man was from a family to which no one in the village paid any attention. Its many members traveled far in search of a living, but they always returned when they sensed the approach of the end. They used to spread out, over there east of the village, along the drainage channel into which the village spills its refuse.

One winter the old man died. He had got his things ready early in the morning and was still in the gallabia in which he had come from the house. The warmth of the sun was still uncertain as he bent over to spread the mat on the stone bench. Then, suddenly, he straightened up and called out to the boy.

At the Roadside

The boy's voice came from behind the shack. He was relieving himself amid the vegetation. The old man slowly walked behind the shack. He lay down facing the sun, turning, searching around with his eyes among the stalks of maize until he saw the boy over there and began to stare at him in silence. The morning dew still moistened the grasses on the edge of the plot of land where the old man had stretched his legs. When the boy returned he found him dead.

The shack remained closed for a day and a night. On the following day another old man came, followed by the boy. The old men in this family all resembled one another; no one in the village was able to distinguish one from another.

Wild Mulberries

We were accustomed to seeing her, that old woman, as we went on our way to the graves. She would be sitting on the bank of the river in her tattered black gallabia, with her basket and stick alongside her. She paid no attention whenever anyone passed along the road, even to those who went up to her to put something in her basket.

In our childhood people would talk about the devils that were always hovering around her, and of the fires that from time to time broke out in the village, and of the children who died strangled and whose bodies floated on the surface of the river.

Despite their warnings and the harsh punishment involved, we would find our way to her. At noon—that time when the streets were empty of grown-ups—we would sneak out. She would receive us with beaming smiles, striking with her stick at the sides of her outstretched legs, and gather us around her. She would allow us to climb the mulberry trees that shaded her, trees that no one before had ever climbed.

Spoilsports would chase us away when we went near one of the trees in the village, warning us that we would fall. Let them come now and see how we were leaping about like monkeys in the branches!

One day the old woman surprised us by producing a piece of rope from her shack. She stood there, restraining her joyful laughter. Then we hurled the end of it over one of the branches and began swinging, while she pushed us and got

Wild Mulberries

taken along with us. She would give whinnying little laughs, her short white hair tumbling about her. She soon tripped up and fell down amid our applause and lay panting for breath outside her shack.

We would slip down to the river, immersing ourselves in it and stretching out our feet on top of the water, then race each other to the other bank. We weren't afraid of the stones that the men of the village threw at us to make us get out of the water, as though in terror of us drowning.

We would find that the old woman, never at a loss for something new, had brought boards of wood and had begun throwing them down to us, those boards on which you could sleep after covering them with straw, and we would jump onto them and use our arms as oars. We would see her running on the bank alongside us, applauding when one of us fell off his board.

When we spotted someone coming along the road, we would rush to her and hide inside her shack and remain there breathless with terror, peeping out through the bamboo poles until they had gone away.

Always something would occur that would keep us from going to the shack. Such periods grew longer as we were taken up with seeking a living.

We set up house, traveled away from the village and returned, had children. And when our children were late coming home, we would search in their faces for traces of mulberry and that gleam that showed they'd been bathing, and through their tears they would swear they hadn't been over there.

We would see her, that old woman, when we passed by her, and it was as though the years had effected no change in her. We would be aware of the uneasy movement of boys inside the shack, yet not one of us would ever dare to go inside and drag them out.

My Grandfather

It was an intensely hot day. On his way back from the market, Grandfather had taken off his outer gown and had slung it over his shoulder. Having reached seventy, he could no longer see more than a few steps ahead of him. The daughter of Suleiman the watchman passed by him, a basket with the ration of oil and sugar on her head and small packets of tea and the ration book in her hand.

"How are you, Uncle Hagg?"[1]

Her gallabia was tattered and, with her raised hand steadying the basket, the curve of her fair-skinned armpit could be seen through its holes.

"Whose daughter are you?"

"Suleiman's."

"Suleiman the watchman."

My grandfather lengthened his stride and walked alongside her. His eyes examined the girl's body and strong bearing. Some days later my grandfather married for the fifth time.

❖

My father was saying: "I thought he'd had enough of this world."

He and my seven uncles were gathered in the room for receiving guests. They had returned early that day, as though by prior arrangement. They had bathed after lunch and had come, as the call to the afternoon prayer was being given, each dressed in a clean gallabia. They were seated on mats, leaning against the couches, with the brazier and the corn cobs in front of them, and the packets of molasses-sweetened

My Grandfather

tobacco. The boys had been forbidden to enter. From outside, the house looked askew. Each time one of my uncles married they would add a number of rooms on the side or at the back. For some reason they had not added another entrance to the house and the heavy wooden door that was always left open remained the sole access. From outside, the house looked more like a long twisting alley off which branched passageways less wide, on both sides of which were the rooms of the uncles. The long alley terminated in a large room where the women would gather each morning for the household chores. The spacious front rooms were given over to Grandfather; always quiet, their floors were covered with colored tiles. The windows were large, and from them was diffused the smell of incense, so beloved of Grandfather. We would remain silent, looking down at the ground, as we passed by them. And when Grandfather moved to another house with his fourth wife, the front rooms stayed empty, not one of my uncles daring to occupy them.

My father would say: "For months I've been watching him. It didn't surprise me. I knew he'd be doing it. When one of them would pass by as he was sitting with us outside, he'd go silent and jerk up his head as he turned toward her. He can't see them from this distance—and yet, praise the Lord."

Says one of my uncles: "She's the age of my daughter."

"Ah."

"And what will people say?"

"And what can they say more than they're saying already?"

"Five times?"

"Ah."

"It would be better for him to marry off his grandchildren."

"Not one of them lasts more than six years with him."

"The fourth stayed for eight and produced no children."

"She lived on for two years, ill."

"May God have mercy upon her."

My Grandfather

They talk for a while and fall silent. They did not talk about the matter for which they had come together. Though they hadn't mentioned it, everyone in the house knew that what was troubling them was the subject of the land. Fifteen years ago, when Grandfather had married for the fourth time, they had gathered—the sons of three wives—in the large inner room. In those days the house had a symmetrical shape, three of my uncles not yet having married. These were seated at a distance from the others. On that day my married uncles, my father among them, had made known their displeasure at Grandfather, for now a year had passed from the death of the third wife. On that day too they had said a lot about things that were shameful and how people were talking, that Grandfather's willfulness had been confirmed, and that things would not end well for him. When in their talk it seemed they were approaching the question of the land, they fell silent and began smoking glumly. This time, too, they didn't speak openly. They had grown older, and stared at length at the coals glowing in the hearth. The land still belonged to Grandfather: he hadn't distributed it to them, though they made a distribution among themselves after the death of Grandfather's fourth wife when they saw him washing his hands of everything and only occasionally passing by the fields. Something like this, though, wasn't to be kept hidden from Grandfather, and often the odd word would slip when they were talking in front of him, one of them saying "my land." Grandfather would nevertheless appear not to have noticed.

Seven years passed with each of them having his land, to which he would go during the day, his children and grandchildren behind him. The grandchildren were now growing up, boys old enough to rummage in the ashes with the end of a straw to collect the small pieces of hot coals for putting on the bowl of the water-pipe.

❖

The wives of my seven uncles, among them my mother, would gather together in the large inner room, having driven out the

My Grandfather

older girls. Their mouths would be turned down, the chairs likewise, all on top of one another in a corner. Sitting on the mats, the women would be dressed in black as though to receive condolences. Ever since the death of Grandfather's fourth wife, they would take it in turns to go to his house, clean it, wash the clothes and prepare him supper—lunch and breakfast he would have with us. After they had had their fill of hurling vilification at his new wife and her father—"that disgusting man who had his greedy eyes on a couple of qirats of land'—a heavy silence would settle over them. What should they do? The young wife was a girl of twenty, what would they call her? How to hold a conversation with her? Would they serve her as they used to do with the fourth wife, who had been older and from a respected family so that my uncles' wives felt no difficulty in cleaning the rooms for her or washing her clothes. She was Grandfather's wife, and Grandfather was never remiss in anything to do with his wife.

❖

Grandfather is with his bride in the small house on the irrigation canal. A many-branched sycamore gives shade to the back of it. Its large green windows are closed throughout the day, while at night a light from inside shows through the slats of the shutters.

Every morning one of my uncles' wives goes to Grandfather's house carrying the tray of food covered with a sheet. They get up early and slit the throats of pigeons and ducks—the birds that Grandfather prefers—bake the bread, and put the soup in the china tureen, with a small plate alongside it containing segments of lime. They would stand around the tray arranging the dishes of food, sprinkling watercress and parsley on the grilled birds and a little ground cinnamon on the dishes of blancmange. They were perplexed over the dish of molasses that Grandfather liked to have with his boiled eggs for breakfast. Some of my uncles' wives considered that it didn't go with the rest of the food, though in the end they put it there and covered it.

My Grandfather

The uncle's wife would return from Grandfather's house bearing the previous day's dirty plates and a bundle of dirty linen. The whole house would gather round her. She would relate that she hadn't seen the bride. It had been Grandfather who had met her and taken the tray from her, and when she had tried to look inside the room she had been met with my Grandfather's stern gaze, so had stood beside the front door until Grandfather himself had gathered up the dirty plates and clothes. She had addressed him in a loud voice in the hope that the bride might appear on hearing her voice, but she didn't.

❖

My seven uncles, together with my father, used to sit on the balcony every afternoon. They would spread out mats, place cushions along the wall, and sprinkle water in front of the house. They would wait for Grandfather to come. They'd keep an eye on the narrow road leading to the irrigation canal which Grandfather was accustomed to take whenever he came to us. The road ended in mulberry trees on both sides, their branches intertwined so that from afar it looks like a dark chasm. Grandfather would make his appearance, suddenly veering off to the side of the road, feeling his way with his stick, stopping, then coming back to the center of the road. After the death of his fourth wife his eyesight had failed badly but he would refuse to allow anyone to accompany him on the way back. From time to time he would come to spend the time around sunset with us, sucking at a couple of lengths of sugar-cane and drinking tea with my uncles around him. He no longer bothered to joke with us, his grandsons, as he used to do when he was living with us.

"I am going now," he would say, and he would remain seated, tapping at the earth with his stick and staring at the roofs of the houses opposite as darkness began to advance upon them.

"Ah, I'm going'—and he would get up in a leisurely manner. At that moment he would appear to have grown old all of a sudden: exceedingly thin and stooping, with a wan

My Grandfather

face, supporting his weight on his stick. With a sigh, he would go sluggishly down the two steps, as he inquired: "He hasn't passed by here?"
"Who?"
He would bow his head for an instant, then move off.
My uncles, my father among them, would sit every day on the balcony from the afternoon until the evening prayer was called, and my father would say: "He won't be coming."
"Ah. Let's perform the evening prayer."

*

Grandfather asked my uncle's wife who had gone to him with the tray of food to send some roast chicken, because his wife didn't like pigeon and duck. The following day he asked my uncle's wife to send some baklava. My father beat his hands together in a gesture of irritation at the thought of having to make a journey to the local town to get it.
"All his life, on every feast day he used to ride to town to eat it and come back."
Grandfather's demands multiplied: the pastries known as *mishaltit*, sugar-cane, lupine seeds, seeds for cracking and munching, peanuts. My uncles' wives were hard at work the whole morning: washing the clothes of Grandfather and his wife, preparing their food, and heating up the bread. There were now all sorts of different kinds of food. They brought a larger tray and even so they had to pack the dishes on it.
"Two of them and they eat all that?" my father would say.
"And who knows whether the girl is eating?"
"How long will it go on?"
"We're on the fourth day."
On the Friday morning Grandfather sent word that he wanted a barber. My father took it as a good omen and said: "He'll be performing the Friday prayer with us."
The barber returned from Grandfather's house after noon. Before going up to the balcony he called out: "God give him a long life. It's amazing, you'd say he'd gone back twenty years. Yes, by God."

My Grandfather

My father asked him whether he would be coming to prayers.

"Of course he'll come," said the barber.

"Did he say so?"

"What would he say to me?"

The midday sun was scorching and the tiled floor of the balcony stung one's feet. My father and my seven uncles were standing awaiting Grandfather. Their eyes were on the road, while sweat poured down their faces. The Friday sermon was almost coming to an end and Grandfather hadn't appeared. One after the other they went down the two steps from the balcony and made their way to the mosque.

❖

It was the hour of afternoon prayer and the sun was still hot. I saw Grandfather as he emerged from the dark shade of the trees wearing a snow-white gallabia with a silk shawl over his shoulders. He was walking in the center of the road with his stick under his arm. A week had passed since he had married. He went up the two stairs with his hand on my head. His face was laughing and glowed in the sunlight. He stood for a moment looking around him and pointed with the stick at the dilapidated parts of the balcony railing: "Where's your father?"

My father and uncles hadn't yet returned. My mother, on hearing his voice, hurried up and bent over his hand. He told her to go to the house to see his wife.

He stood at the entrance to the hallway leaning on his stick. His tall frame had filled out, his shoulders drawn back. My mother went off, concealing her laughter in her head-dress. Grandfather looked inside the hallway for a while, then came out and walked away in the direction of the market.

❖

My mother said that the girl was in a bad way and that her health was deteriorating.

My Grandfather

She was carrying a bundle of clothes under her arm. She passed by my father and uncles who were sitting in the hallway awaiting her return from Grandfather's house. She said nothing else.

Every day she went to Grandfather's house. She would spend the afternoon there—those hours when Grandfather had left the house. As for the tray of food, it would go at the fixed time every morning, and my mother would do the washing there and return with a glum expression and go off straight away to our rooms.

One day my father stopped her in front of the hallway and asked: "What's the news?"

"By the Prophet," she said, "I'm at a loss, Abu Salim. The girl doesn't complain of a thing, but every day she's in a bad way."

❖

My father placed the plush saddle on the mule and tied it up in front of the balcony.

"It's for Grandfather when he comes," he said.

Grandfather came in the afternoon, mounted the mule, unfurled the parasol, and went off to the fields. His shouting carried over long distances. He had taken off his shoes, folded the parasol, and raised his gallabia over his thighs. My uncles were gathered around him, while others came along from the nearby plots of land. They were walking in a throng amid the plots of land: it was as though the days of old had returned. They all ended up eventually in the shade of the willow trees, sitting around in a circle with Grandfather presiding, having brought with them sugar-cane, lettuces, and tomatoes.

❖

It was the hour of sunset. I was standing on the bank of the irrigation canal looking at Grandfather's house. The house was set slightly aside from the other houses. The yellow light of the sun was touching the branches of the sycamore tree that leaned over the back of the house. Hanging on the

My Grandfather

clothes-line on the roof were a green gallabia and some of Grandfather's underclothes. Despite my uncle's warning against any one of us grandchildren going there, I approached the house. The front door was open and I saw her standing in the gap: thin in a long gallabia. She wore her hair in a plump pigtail. Her face was emaciated, her cheeks sunken. She was leaning her shoulder against the side of the door, staring out at the gushing waters of the canal. Suddenly, as though sensing my presence, she turned. Her eyes passed over me and it was as though she wasn't seeing me. Then she again looked at me for a moment, and when she motioned me to approach I moved away.

❖

Grandfather's wife died at dawn. My mother had spent the night with her, and Grandfather had come after the doctor had left and had sat with my uncles in the hall, and they had lit the mantle-lamp. Around midnight they had stretched out around him and fallen asleep. He had remained sitting with his back to the couch and his arm stretched over his knee, closing his eyes from time to time.

When the screaming broke out at the canal, he got to his feet and stood on the balcony.

---

[1] 'Uncle' is a term of address used to someone older. 'Hagg,' i.e. someone who has performed the pilgrimage, is used as a term of respect.

A Last Glass of Tea

The mother placed the kettle amid the embers in the hearth. She looked with eyes watery from the smoke at her son in the far corner. The light was faint in the room and from behind the closed door came the sound of a child crying and a woman shouting.
"Your wife hasn't slept," said the mother.
She opened a box beside her and took out a blue woolen gallabia. She passed her hand over it for a while and said, "Your wedding gallabia. Wear it."
She took out a white silk scarf, which she threw to him. He put on the gallabia and placed the scarf on his shoulder. She gazed at him for an instant and inclined her head to the wall. This burdensome waiting had suddenly come to an end. Her face looked pale in the light of the fire.
"Your wife was wanting to keep the gallabia in her wardrobe."
She took from the box a rifle, which she passed to him. He was handling it when it occurred to him that everything that was now happening was not unfamiliar to him. A slender line of steam was rising from the mouth of the kettle, with the sound of the water boiling inside. On that day his father had said, "The kettle's boiling."
He had said it in a whisper, his face to the wall. The horse had been neighing outside, the wind blowing strongly, and the moon luminous.
"It's a full moon," his mother had said.
He was a young lad sitting beside the hearth fighting off sleep, with the warmth flowing into his bare feet. His father

A Last Glass of Tea

was standing in the middle of the reception room, stretching his arms into the woolen gallabia, and his mother was handing him the rifle, when his father had turned round. The color of his face was wanly yellow in the light of the lamp, his eyes blankly staring, his mustache thick and unkempt.

"The kettle's boiling," he had whispered.

His mother, who had been arranging the shawl on his father's back, had bent over and moved the kettle away from the live coals.

"Just bring her," she had said. "Don't touch so much as a hair on her head."

His father was walking ahead of the two of them, his head lowered against the cold gusts of wind. He himself tripped along clinging to the body of his mother who had flung her arm over him. His father had untied the horse from the sycamore tree and mounted it. He had remained silent. His mother had placed the two bundles of provisions and the water in front of him and had stood beside him.

"If things are as you say ...," he whispered, leaning down a little.

"They are as I said."

"It didn't happen at all."

"But it did."

He saw the lizards glinting in the bright moonlight on the walls, and the windows of the houses closed, their rusted iron a dark color, and the piles of straw and dry maize on the flat roofs, their ends bending with the wind.

He walked with his mother behind the horse. His father had wrapped the shawl round his face and head. He seemed no longer to be aware of the two of them. When his mother coughed, his head inclined a little toward them and he said, "Go back."

They came out of the alleys into open country. His mother was dragging him by the shoulders as the wind stung his ears and his father was moving away. His mother hurried along, and he with her, though he saw nothing; his face was hidden

A Last Glass of Tea

in the folds of her gallabia, and the noise of the wind dominated all other sounds. He heard his father's shout circling above them, "Go back."

And his mother shouting, "Don't touch her. Just bring her back."

He didn't see him as he ascended the hill and confronted the desert. The neighing of the horse as it made the descent was carried away by the winds. Nevertheless his mother, who had remained standing in the open country until he had disappeared on the other side of the hill, used to recount later: "He was over there on top of the hill, and the moonlight was all around him. He was looking at us. Perhaps he was saying something. I didn't hear him."

He was clasping her leg, with the wind sweeping the open country, and she drew him back with her. All the time she was mumbling words he could not make out. From the way her hand was grasping his shoulder, he sensed that she wouldn't notice if he were to cry.

"He's been away for a whole day and night," said his mother. She was sitting in the courtyard with her back to the wall and her women neighbors with her. He was lying down with his head on her thigh when he saw the neck of the horse at the opening of the door. It was breathing heavily and licking at the side of the lintel. He heard his mother's scream and her hand striking her breast. The man who had brought the horse was standing by in confusion. He allowed the reins to fall from his hand. He said that he had come across it by the hill. His mother snatched up the rifle attached to the saddle and placed it in the box. Later, he was to see her through the open door of the room taking it out and wiping it with a cloth moistened in oil, then wrapping it up and replacing it in the box.

His mother poured the tea into the glass and pushed the brazier to one side. He became aware of the sound of the wind outside and the heavy breathing of the horse tethered to the bars of the window. He was sitting on the couch his

A Last Glass of Tea

father used to sit on. His mother placed the glass of tea on a tray in front of him. She had never talked about his sister before.

"You were young," she said. "Do you remember her?"

He wanted to say that he did. Her eyes were staring into his, and he kept silent.

She used to stand in front of the piece of mirror hanging on the wall of the reception room, combing her hair, which she had just washed. Light drops of water stung his face as she sharply drew the comb through. He was lying in bed watching her. Her breast was taut, confined by the gallabia, its collar always open at the back. Her neck looked thin and long, covered with blond fluff that extended as far as her shoulder blades.

He would awake from sleep to the touch of her hands as she wrapped him round in the covering, and he would see the sparkle of her eyes, like those of cats, in the darkness. When she sensed that he was awake, she would tickle him under the arms. She slept little at night. She would brush the cover off with her feet and stand behind the closed window, and he would feel the sting of cold when she got up from beside him. She would remain standing with her flimsy nightgown and bare shoulders as she listened to the sound of the wind and the faraway barking of dogs. Sometimes she would wake him with a faint whispering and ask him to tell her about the boys he had played with in the morning and the people he had seen. She would listen for a while, then he would sense, as her hand stopped stroking his head, that she was no longer listening to him. That was before the gypsy came to the village. On that day he had been playing with the boys in the lane and they had seen him coming. Breathless, they had stopped their play and looked at him. He had been riding an old horse and held in his lap a lamb born two days ago. Behind him was his wife on a mule with a saddlebag, both sides of which were filled, and leading another mule loaded with baggage; round about the two of them was a flock of goats and sheep enveloped in a thick

A Last Glass of Tea

cloud of dust. He was tall and robust with a radiant face that shone in the sunlight, and had locks of black hair as curly as a sheep's fleece and sleepy eyes that lightly took note of the passers-by. His wife looked skinny and as dried up as firewood, with wrinkles round her mouth. They said in the village that they had not changed since the last time they had come, two years ago. They said she was his mother, then, later, that she was his wife and that she was barren. However, for some reason or other, he did not leave her. With those gypsies no one knows what goes on between them. On the previous occasion they had stayed on in the village for three months. They walked along the same streets and alleys until they ended up at the hill, and it was there that they had pitched their tent. The woman had driven in the pegs and stretched out the ropes between two bowed date-palms that gave shade to the tent, while the goats and sheep were scattered about the open country.

It seemed that the spectacle of the old woman and her young man had attracted the attention of the women in the village. They would go up to the rooftops at night and hold their gatherings, looking down at the hill and talking about what they could see down there in the lighted tent, and about the old woman, whose mewing sounds could be heard in the open country. They would say, "Poor thing—after all these years of life to be without a child."

They would say it with malicious laughter. Seeing how ugly the old woman was and the way the gypsy stuck to her, they would block his way in the alleys as he passed and bombard him with remarks.

"Brother, what a lot of sheep you've got—may the Lord increase them."

"May the Prophet keep you as young as ever!"

His face would scowl slightly under the pressure of their gaze and he would make off without turning to them.

His mother stands leaning with her elbows on the wall of the flat roof. His sister is sitting on the last step of the stairs

A Last Glass of Tea

after his mother has scolded her and told her to go away. He passed by her, coming close to his mother. The moon was hidden behind the clouds. In the semi-darkness he could make out women sitting among the piles of straw on the roofs of neighboring houses. He clung to the wall beside his mother, though she drove him away. He went off and then returned and hung on the wall near to her and looked where the women were looking. The tent was there under the hill: a luminous path amid a wide expanse of darkness. A lighted lamp was hanging in the middle of the tent, and he saw in the spread of light sheep lying down in front of the tent and a dark shadow moving inside, the head lowered in order to avoid the hanging lamp. The light was flickering with the wind and the fabric of the tent rippled. The place looked like many scenes that came to him in dreams. He couldn't make it out at all: soft and slightly rocking, always seeming to be about to vanish. It looked, from the movement of the shadow, that he was taking off his waistcoat. For a moment he stood there naked, then he leaned away out of sight. He saw the old woman as she entered the tent and stood in the center. She undid the head-dress and took off the gallabia: it was doubtless the long black gallabia in which she had arrived. It seemed from her shadow that she was putting on another less voluminous gallabia. She looked more like a boy, though she had suddenly spread out her hair. She had let it loose with her hands in a swift movement, bending her head back so that her hair fell down, long and plentiful. She stretched out her hand to the lamp and the light died, becoming a small red circle. There was a slight movement among the women on the neighboring roof-tops. He saw them getting up and brushing off the remnants of straw clinging to their gallabias as they noiselessly disappeared. His mother also turned round and made her way down the staircase.

He would go up to the roof in the twilight of dawn before washing his face and hang onto the wall and stare down at the ewes. He would see them crouched all together, covering

A Last Glass of Tea

a great patch of land around the tent like small mounds of manure. How many times he had tried to count them! He would see the gypsy coming from behind the tent where the hill was, his chest bare and a shawl round his neck. He would untether the horse and the two mules and lead them to the river. At the same time his sister would emerge carrying the washbowl filled with the cooking pots to wash them in the river. He would hear the creaking of the front door and would wait for a time, then see her on the road leading to the river. After that the shouting of Salim's wife could be heard. His mother would say that she was always quarrelsome. He could see her husband in the open courtyard as, with hands and feet, he struck at her, then dragged her and hurled her outside. She would curl up on the stone bench outside the house, sobbing in a low voice. The morning light would glow, the red disc of the sun appearing behind the hill, and he would see the gypsy returning from the river riding his horse, with the two mules behind him. After that his sister would come, walking in the wet tracks left behind by the horse and the mules on the earth of the road.

"And I see her with my very eyes," his mother would wail.

He stood alongside her on the roof. This time she was not aware of him. He saw the tent lighted up and the gypsy's shadow moving. He was carrying some things, transporting them from one place to another. The shadow of his wife appeared bowed. The wind was quiet and the ewes bunched up in the lighted space, while the goats remained unsettled, coming from the darkness, standing for a moment in the light, then vanishing. The women on the roof opposite were whispering together, then all of a sudden fell silent. A third shadow had appeared inside the tent. It stood quietly in the entrance. From the way the upper half protruded it appeared to be a woman whose head and shoulders were encircled by a wrap. The gypsy's wife rose to her feet and passed beside her to the outside. The gypsy approached her and stood in

A Last Glass of Tea

front of her, removing the wrap from her head. His arm stayed on her shoulder, then he drew her inside and put out the lamp.

It was a moonlit night and the gypsy's wife was walking among the ewes and feeling their heads. Then she squatted down among them. When he turned his gaze to her again he was unable to make her out, though he could see—after the light had vanished—the goats standing nearby around the mounds of sleeping ewes. The women suddenly exchanged cries on the roof opposite as they struck out at each other, laughing. His mother, too, laughed, and the women hastened to the stairway.

"And I see her with my very eyes," his mother used to wail in a whisper.

She rested her head wound round in black against the wall; her eyes were dry, her lips the color of ashes. He was calling to her and went on for a time calling to her until she turned to him. She looked him up and down.

His wife was giving birth in the room, with the women coming and going, and he saw her sitting in the corner of the courtyard on a heap of straw. When the midwife came out of the reception room his mother's eyes were fixed on her.

The midwife went up to her and whispered, "A boy."

He hadn't seen her crying before. Suddenly she rose to her feet and disappeared.

She took the boy to live in her room. She would call his wife to suckle him. He is aware of her light tapping at the door of his room at night in order to waken his wife, and he hears the soft grumbling of his wife on her return. She said to him one day, "Your mother's changed a lot. Had I known I'd have brought her the boy a year ago." His mother said, "You've grown up and become a man."

The boy was stretched out on her thigh, his back naked to the sun. He stood in front of her in silence. Her face looked like a piece of rock. In the light of the sun she had lowered her eyes slightly, while her hand stroked the back of the boy, who

A Last Glass of Tea

had begun to climb up her stomach. As he was going away, her voice came to him, soft and tender, as she sang to the boy.

She was standing with the boy on her shoulder, and he crossed the courtyard on his way to the front door. It was afternoon.

"Don't go out tonight," she said, and she went off with the boy to her room.

Slender wisps of blue smoke rose from the tray of coals. Some live embers slipped down to its blackened rim, their glow almost dead. His mother was putting them back among the burning coals with her fingernail. With his eyes he followed the thin thread of smoke. Every time it appeared as if he were seeing the ceiling for the first time: the projecting wooden beams that had grown black with smoke; the dangling wire for hanging the pressure-lamp, its thickness increased by the spiders' webs, which had been effaced by the accumulated soot; and a small aperture carved out of the wall close to the ceiling, where he saw the old pressure-lamp leaning.

He became aware of his mother's voice. "She's grown up now. Perhaps she has children."

She was turning over the coals with her finger.

"When you see her you'll know her. Like all the family her features, however old she is, won't have changed."

Her dry lips partly slightly: it was as though she were smiling.

"All these years. Your father used to sit where you are. He never understood. That night he started to cry and say 'How could it be?' If only he'd listened to what I told him and gone after her. I didn't find her at dawn. I waited to hear the sound of the cooking-pots as she gathered them up into the washing bowl. Every time I was on the roof I'd see the shadow and I'd say to myself that it wasn't unfamiliar. I'd tell your father to catch up with them before they disappeared amid the tribes. He didn't want to go at all. All the time he was saying 'How could it be?' After that I knew he wasn't able to face people.

A Last Glass of Tea

He didn't look me in the eyes; he would talk to me as if I wasn't beside him. He would say, 'Let's sell the land and go away.' And he would say, 'I'll go away for two or three years and come back to you.' I'd say to him, 'Let my daughter return home and after that do what you wish.' He said I was mad and that I was the reason for all the misfortune."

With the tip of her finger she brushed the crumbly ash off the coals.

"If only he'd listened to what I told him."

She passed him the last glass of tea and put the kettle to one side. She pulled out the black shawl from above a basket behind her. She shook it out and let it remain on her outstretched leg. He wanted to say that too many years had passed. It seemed she had noticed something on his face. Her look was fleeting and she inclined her head toward the coals.

"I used to say that you were different from your father. If only she had died, there would have been an end of the matter. Tell her to come back. Don't touch her."

It was a moonlit night and dawn had begun to stream into the horizon. The wind quieted slightly. She was walking beside him, her hand on the horse's hindquarters. When they got out into open country, the wind grew stronger.

"Go back," he said to her.

Spurring the horse forward, he ascended the hill. Turning round, he saw her over there in the middle of the empty open space, enveloped in black at the same spot on which the gypsy had set up his tent. The horse neighed as it went down to the desert.

On the Brink

Usually I would see the two of them in the courtyard of the house: the boy, covered with black hair, would be crawling along happily, while my wife would be clapping her hands and laughing, her full, naked breast showing through the opening of the gallabia. The boy, letting out a shout, would hurl himself onto the heap of straw. He would roll over and over, then get up and dash to her.

Half the courtyard was covered over with palm branches and sacking. The other half, toward the house, had been left open. It would be immersed in the morning's warm sunshine and my wife would sit there cross-legged at this hour in front of the baking oven, and sometimes in front of the bowl in which she did the washing. She would shake the flour or the soap suds from her hands, and the boy would come toward her, wisps of straw in his body hair, his small, sharp eyes fixed on her breast, which she would shake lightly with her hand. His teeth were snowy-white amid the thick black hair that covered his face. He would lie back in her lap, his hands holding her breast and his feet scraping against the ground. Suddenly he would spit out the nipple and turn his face round toward me, as though aware of me standing at the threshold of the courtyard. He raised himself slightly, supporting his weight with his elbows on her thigh, then once again went back to her breast.

The day of his birth the midwife had rushed out of the room making trilling sounds of joy. She approached me: "A blessing—one of the saints of God."

On the Brink

The men and the women in the courtyard uttered expressions of praise to the Almighty. "Sheikh Ahmad," they said. "We shall call him Sheikh Ahmad."

He is now five years old. He still sucks at his mother's breast, which dried up years ago. In his moments of exuberance he enjoys crawling around in the courtyard and taking hold of rounded objects, which he gnaws with his teeth, then throws away if he doesn't find them pleasant. He stops moving about when I pass him and remains staring expectantly with his gleaming eyes. He doesn't approach me to play, as though sensing my aversion to him, and when his small bell rolls toward me he stays standing where he is until I have gone away.

The boys in the lane don't linger long in front of oddities. They would call to him to come and play, and they would never, even in their quarrels, refer to his appearance. The most they would do was make fun of him for still sucking at his mother's breast, and when they saw him stopping play in order to scratch his body violently, they would seat him on the stone bench and lift up his gallabia and gather around him while they searched for the insects that had invaded his thick hair.

His mother, too, after giving him suck, would spread him out on her lap and comb through his body hair with the delouser. Sometimes she would plunge him into the water of the washing-bowl for the insects to float to the surface; he would get out of the bowl with the water dripping from him and his black body-hair would look soft and sleek, gleaming in the light of the sun as he stood there drying off.

The barber would come on a Friday before prayers. He would sit him on a flat stone in the courtyard and cover his body in lather and run the razor over him from tip to toe: the heaving, scraping sound of the blade, the boy silent, and the barber squatting on his heels and circling round him. When he came to his face the movement of the razor would grow slower as it passed lightly round the eyes and lips.

When the barber left, the boy would stand contemplating his body as though seeing it as something strange. He would

On the Brink

touch it again and again, leaning sideways in an attempt to look at his back. He would run to his mother, who would kiss his stomach and laugh.

When the hair grows he cannot bear the gallabia on his body and his mother makes do with a pair of short trousers in which he wanders around all the time, his hand scratching at every part of his body, while from time to time he rushes off to his mother for her to scratch his back.

I wake at night to the sound of faint singing. His mother is rocking him. He is curled up trembling in her lap. Those moonlit nights when the moon shines and illuminates the courtyard. The silvery light is reflected on the glass of the window and faint shadows ripple on the wall of the reception room, appearing and disappearing. I wake up to the deep silence outside and the croaking of distant frogs. The boy's eyes are shining in the semi-darkness. He is staring toward me as I lie on the couch facing the bed where he sleeps with his mother. I turn my face to the wall.

The rain comes and goes. It continues for days, inundating the courtyard. Sometimes the sky is clear: the sparkle of moonlight on the mud, the crevices filled with water. The boy stands at the threshold to the courtyard. My wife watches him through the open door of the reception room. She tosses and turns in the warmth of the bed. "Can you see?" she whispers. "The hair keeps him warm."

I was put off by the woman. She would come and go, hurrying after him with food, the front of her gallabia always open. She would lay him down on her thighs and rock him till he went to sleep, his hand buried in her bosom. And in bed she would take him to her and continue for a time kissing his head and stroking his back. I would look at her naked stomach and ask myself how it had become filled with such a one. Out of the corner of her eye she would watch me as she combed her wet hair, turning round and staring into my face. I would be lying on the couch and the boy would be deep asleep. She would stand in front of me with her flimsy gallabia drawn tightly

On the Brink

round her body, showing the roundness of her belly, as though to excite me—that belly that I hated. I would find myself looking at her in astonishment, as though blaming her for trying.

She or any other woman. I would see them in the jostle of the market-place: beautiful faces moist with sweat. I used to say that nothing so attracted me as a beautiful face moist with sweat, a slight tiredness in the eyes as though longing for shade and sparkling water. I pass by them and see the sweat on their faces as lines in the midst of viscid earth. And what do they carry in their bellies? She used to grasp my face between her hands and bring it into contact with her swollen belly and I would listen to the child's moving inside her, striking out in every direction. For long months I had listened. I would lie down and listen and her voice would murmur softly: "Can you hear him?"

And I would find myself drawn to the concealed voices within.

Nothing arouses my anger, I am never upset. My voice might be raised but I am soon in control of myself. I see things as proceeding without fuss, day after day: one year comes to an end and another begins. I come back from the school to find my food on the table in the reception room, covered over with a cloth, and I hear her laughter in the courtyard. My bed is made; my gallabia is hanging up. All my things are in their place. I say to myself: "What do I lack?"

My nature is calm and secretive. No one can guess what is going on inside me. I am used to conversing with people while thinking at the same time about something else. I stand before the students in class, explaining the lesson and answering their questions, and I bring to mind the two of them over there in the courtyard playing together. She runs after him to catch him. A gleam of joy lights up her face. He is in his shorts. She stops him and removes the straw and dirt that is adhering to his hair. His eyes alight on the ladder leaning against the wall. He slips from her grasp and hurries toward it. He climbs up it to the roof. Taking hold of a beam jutting

On the Brink

out from the ceiling, he lets his body dangle. He swings by it, while she shouts and wails, spreading out her arms. She asks me: "Why don't you put him into the school?"

The teachers, too, ask me that. I say to myself: "Doesn't it seem odd to them? Are they humoring me? It's been going on for years. A few months after his birth I would hear of the jokes they exchanged. For a while they remained at a loss to determine the sort of animal that my wife had had intercourse with, for there were no monkeys in the district. And now they are pressing me to put him in the school. Perhaps my own attitude seemed strange to them, I who had so wanted the boy. For three months—ever since I heard the movement of him in her womb—I was imagining the day when he would accompany me to school, following me along the road, his satchel dangling at his side. He walks half a pace from me. I open the sunshade and he clings to me so that we might both be in its shade. He widens his stride so as to keep up with me. On seeing a dog barking he clutches at my clothes. I always imagined him to be frightened of barking dogs. I tell him not to pay any attention and that they'll go away. In the break he rushes into the school courtyard in search of me. I'm standing with the teachers. I feel him taking hold of my hand and standing silently by me.

❖

It was a hot day and the sun had been flooding the courtyard of the house from early morning. The small chicks were lying in the shade alongside the wall. The boy was jumping about in his shorts, which his mother had made for him from an old gallabia of hers. I called out for him to follow me. Then I stopped short uncertainly. It came as a surprise to me, for it had not happened before that I had taken him out with me. It was as though something was growing inside me without my realizing. And now that the matter has been decided, I feel the tremor that had swept over me disappear and I am wet with sweat. I was out of sight beside the door, far from the gaze of my wife who had begun to look for me, with the boy romping around her and pointing in my direction. She was dressing

On the Brink

him in a gallabia, then she turned and our eyes met. Was she guessing what was going on inside me? I stretched out my foot in the face of the grey cat, the boy's friend, which was trying to enter. It, too, would make an appearance in my imaginings in the long nights of sleeplessness. I would see it squatting on the fence, its mewing following me as I steal into the courtyard and stand by the head of the boy, who would be lying on his stomach on the pile of straw. Turning toward me, it would shake its head. For an instant it would meet my glance, then quietly crawl away, its body alert as though smelling danger.

I walked with the boy walking alongside me. He extended his stride to keep up with me.

He asked me if his gallabia was clean.

I told him it was.

We left the village behind us. The boy looked at my face from time to time. Perhaps he wanted to ask about where we were going but feared that this would make me angry.

We come to a stop at the canal lock. The waters of the river surge darkly, crashing against the iron lock gate. The boy is at my side talking about his friends who are older and who come at noon to bathe and who hang on to the lock gate and then jump and pass under it. When he grows up he will come with them. I listen for a while to the roar of the waters under my feet. I look around me and see no one. The boy is still talking about his friends and throwing pebbles into the water. I hear him laugh. The light of the sun between the branches of the tree veils my eyes. The sound of his laughter comes as though he had gone far away. Once again I look around me. I push him. I hear, as I turn around, the faint scream and the sound of his striking the water. I hurry away. The noise of the water thunders in my ears, the sun hurts my eyes.

Approaching the village, I walked more slowly. Looking behind me, I saw him coming. Naked, he was squeezing out his gallabia. He came to a stop when he saw me looking at him. He continued to squeeze out his gallabia. I regarded him for a while. I was calm. I went on walking and he walked behind me.

The Hill

There is something dreamlike about the scene.

The hill looks as though the waters of the sea have only recently pulled back from it. It is flooded by the sunset light. Its white sands are washed clean. They have a listless sparkle. The winds blow and take away the soft dust that clings to them. Vast untrodden tracts have retained a brittle crust of sand; though containing slight cracks they remain cohesive. Dark green splodges of grasses and thorn bushes, round which lizards dart. A few small houses scattered on the hill. From the irregular way in which they have been constructed, they appear to have been made by their owners. Their doors are of corrugated iron and are always left ajar. One of them is far off, all on its own. It looks down on the incline that leads to the sea. A black nanny goat is tied to a stake in front of it, with children playing close by. They choose flat stones and hurl them at the sea. When the woman comes out of the house, they disperse.

It was at her usual time and the sun was almost setting. She was wearing a black gallabia with a black headscarf. There was white in the parting of her hair where the headscarf had slipped slightly. Undoing the goat's tether, she took it into the house. She went down the slope by a narrow, crumbling footpath covered with large and small white stones. On her way down she encountered gusts of wind that impeded her movements and made her bend over from time to time, the gallabia wrapping itself around her thin body.

The sea is violently clamorous. Flat, slippery rocks are struck by the waves. The footpath ends at a narrow strip of

The Hill

small black rocks which have remained dry. Sometimes the spray from a tall wave reaches it, flowing down from between its cracks to the large flat rocks.

Boats are lined up upside down on the sands below the hill. Their prows rest on small black rocks. The woman walks to two boats in the center that have been placed facing each other and have split open slightly like two shells. She seats herself between them on a white stone she had brought one day from the footpath. The sound of the sea reverberates deeply in the emptiness of them, and soft white sand and grasses and small empty tins have piled up inside. The woman takes out of her pocket some dried dates. Waiting until a wave pulls away, she throws one after another into it.

"Mercies upon him. A thousand mercies upon him—on him who returned and on him who didn't."

The sea appeared to have become rougher. Its tall waves strike violently against the rocks, then retreat in spray topped with spume. In their pursuit of one another the waves strive to pass beyond the rocks as though to reach the hill itself. The hill seems to tower, fluorescent in the sunset. In the evening glow the white sands take on the color of ears of wheat, in their extensiveness undulating like tiny motionless waves, with wide gaps in which the shadows are as heavy as scars. The dark balls of grasses sway with the wind and a soft cloud of dust moves around the hill from time to time, taking on its way the grasses that have fallen down and throwing them into the gaps.

The woman wipes away the spray that sprinkles her face. She spreads out her legs. It is the first time the waters have touched her feet and wetted the hem of her gallabia. There is a sound she has not heard before: a deep, suppressed rumble on the point of explosion. She sees the wave approaching, advancing menacingly. She watches it, smiling. She gathers the gallabia round her thighs and arranges her headscarf. Hardly has she done so than the sound booms out: a vast dark barrier. She floats: her feet touch the smooth, slippery rocks.

The Hill

The two boats alongside her rise up, then break into pieces. She turns round, laughing. She stretches out her hand to her headscarf, which has soared away. Her eyes are shining, her laughter short and noisy, her short wet hair in disarray about her face. She slips and rolls down. Suddenly she straightens up breathlessly into a sitting position. She rises and falls with the jutting of the huge rocks. Vainly she strikes the water with her hands as she disappears amid the folds of the waves. At last darkness descends. A low rumbling emanates from deep inside the sea and small restive waves lick at the sides of the rocks.

Drought

Date-palms stood thick around the village, stretching far into the open country. The two men left the darkness of the date-palms and walked into the open country. The tall man left first, wearing a black shirt and light shoes. Turning round, he saw the other man approaching. After that he didn't turn round. The other man was wearing a dark-colored gallabia and had a dirty white shawl round his head. The distance between them remained constant.

It was an extensive area of wasteland covered with numerous crevices and dried-up water channels, along the sides of which were scattered thorns and thin leafless trees, their branches looking like sticks for firewood. The sun's glare was fierce and there was a hot wind that carried with it powdery dust.

They crossed over the wasteland heading toward a green patch that showed up from afar. They walked deliberately, as though the wind was impeding their progress; the man in front leant forward, the other had placed his shawl about his mouth and nose. The air was colored a pale yellow, the sun covered over with a turbid coating.

The green patch rose slightly above the ground and the man disappeared into it. The other was still striding behind him in the dust-storm, his gallabia wrapped tightly around his body.

The man walked along a narrow watercourse, on the sides of which were dark green thorn bushes tipped with

Drought

yellow flowers. Thickly-branched trees began to shake in the wind. The canal ended in a cement barrier, after which the land sloped down toward open country. He turned at the sound of faint footsteps and appeared to have been caught unawares by the other man at the side of the watercourse. In silence they exchanged glances.

The whirlwinds were chasing each other beyond the trees, sweeping away the dried thorn-bushes with them as they went. The man in the gallabia bent over and washed his face, drying it with the end of his scarf. Then he crossed the watercourse. He was short and had the face of an old man, with a thick black mustache and small eyes. The other, the man with the black shirt, was clean-shaven, with the face of a child; he smoothed back his hair from his eyes as he breathed heavily, his back against the trunk of a tree.

The wind increased in violence, the sound of it echoing emptily among the trees. The glare of the sun disappeared; its weak light still penetrated through from time to time, the air smelling of the dark-colored dust.

The short man placed his hands into the side openings of his gallabia: he appeared to be smoothing out his waistcoat. He took a step forward and the young man's hands shook slightly, then remained in repose by his sides. His face was moist with sweat and dust.

The man rushed at him quickly, lunging at the young man's stomach, turning his hand from left to right. For the instant the young man looked as though he had been taken by surprise; his hands took hold of the man's fist and he leaned over noiselessly. He was slowly slipping down, his head falling onto the man's shoulder; as he made a further effort, his head remained where it was. The man withdrew his fist and the young man's body twitched; the man grasped him under the arms and gently lowered him. The young man collapsed in a heap, turning over on his back, then crawled forward a little until he was up against the trunk of the tree. He let out a gasp, then became limp and silent.

Drought

Dry leaves covered the place, clinging to the tips of the thorn-bushes and floating on the surface of the watercourse. Removing some with his hand, the man washed his knife and returned it to his pocket, then set off back.

The violence of the wind had lessened, though the air remained redolent with the smell of dust.

A Weak Light Revealing Nothing

They were over there amid the tall eucalyptus trees, which, with their dense shadows, formed a triangle on the river bank. They had no doubt come by night, for no one had seen them arrive, nothing indicating their presence except for a cannon on two wheels standing beyond the trees, its muzzle aimed upward, and two soldiers mounted on horses blocking off the bridge leading to the village.

The fishermen returning at dawn were the first to see them. The rags they wore when they were wading in the lake were still wet and they carried on their backs the nets and baskets of fish. They passed by the cannon without noticing it, but when they went up the road to the bridge they were stopped by the two soldiers. At first they thought they were patrolmen. There were four of them and they stood in silence waiting to hear what the soldiers would say. However, the two soldiers pushed forward toward them on their horses. The four men scattered like frightened sheep. The soldiers, waving their sticks, trapped them between the horses and began prodding at them with the ends of the sticks. The fishermen retreated, protesting loudly; they continued to back away until they reached the trees, where they came to a stop. When they saw that the soldiers were bent on pursuing them, they darted off among the trees.

❖

A Weak Light Revealing Nothing

Owais, the railroad switch operator, left his shack and made his way to the village to perform the dawn prayer in the mosque. Although there were various ruined buildings and water-channels on the way which lent themselves as places in which to relieve himself, he preferred to do so in the trees, for the water-channel there was lined with cement. "Beautiful cement—and the water's beautiful. You can see it as it flows."

The ground, too, was clean and free of weeds, so he could see the snakes and frogs and avoid them.

He, too, did not see the cannon. He walked through the trees until he reached the water-channel. When they surrounded him, he was tracing lines with his finger in the dust. He looked at them and was incapable of rising to his feet.

❖

We were on the river bank, knowing they had come, and we gazed around for them. They were on the other bank, hidden by the dark shadows of the trees; the cannon was beyond them, glinting in the sunlight.

"A revolution? What revolution?"

Our village was small and isolated. Like others, we had heard of the revolution taking place, then had forgotten about it—even the headmaster of the village's only preparatory school. The picture of the king had remained in his office and he had paid it no attention until the revolution actually reached the village. The teachers and pupils gathered in the courtyard, cheering and demanding to go to the river. The headmaster left his office, went down the two steps, and walked to the gate and opened it, shouting, "Off you go!"

Then, returning to his office, he took down the picture and hid it among the files on the shelf. He was rushing across the courtyard when the flag caught his eye. He dashed toward it, remembering that the revolution had brought with it a new flag. He seized the flagpole from its socket and carried it and the flag to the store-room, and hurried to catch up with the others.

❖

A Weak Light Revealing Nothing

In those moments before we went to the river, it was as though a storm had swept over the village. People were running and shouting through the alleys, and the shops and houses were closed. Al-Adawi stood in front of his house, striking the palm of one hand against the other, saying, "Glory be to God!"

And his wife, standing behind him, repeated, "Glory be to God!"

When the turmoil in the alley had died down, they hurried inside and locked the door. Al-Adawi dug with his hands in the corner of the inner reception room, after moving the breadbox to one side, and extracted a small tin.

"What a strong smell it's got!" said his wife.

"Give me a rag."

He wrapped the tin in the rag and placed it under his arm, and the two of them left. They hurried along the empty lanes in the opposite direction to the river and reached a narrow alley that led to the fields behind the village. Omran appeared, coming from the other direction. Even before they met up, he called out, "Where are you going to, Adawi? Everyone's going to the river."

"Yes, I'll be going."

He stood in front of them. His nose picked up the smell of the hashish.

"Are you really going?"

He stared at them and a slight tremor ran through his immense, flabby body, while his bulging eyes came to rest on the packet.

"Ah, Adawi—for ten days now you've not been giving me any. Have I been a day late in paying what I owe?"

"Never, Omran. I'm not happy about you, though. You were smoking too much."

"And where are you taking it?"

"They say they'll be searching the houses."

"And even if they do, how many times have they searched your house before? Twenty? And what did they find?"

A Weak Light Revealing Nothing

He laughed and leaned across al-Adawi, poking him in the side.

"So, what did they find?"

Al-Adawi laughed. The two of them suddenly burst out laughing. Omran said, breathing heavily, "What do you say about the plain-clothes men?"

"A lot of bastards."

"How many times did they search your house?"

"Many times."

"And how do they search?"

"They turn everything upside down."

"Fine—and what did they find?"

"And what have I got for them to find?"

"Quite right. And what have you got?"

His eyes went back to examining the packet under al-Adawi's arm.

"What's it weigh?"

"Nothing at all—just a couple of finger-lengths."

"More. Let me weigh it in my hand."

Al-Adawi retreated a step. He pushed his wife in front of him, and the two of them moved off: a tall, exceedingly thin man, his voluminous gallabia trailing the ground behind him, and his short, plump wife, her black *milaya* round her shoulders.

"He saw us, Adawi."

"And even if he did. I only wish all the people of the village were like him. He's the only one I never cheat."

They approached the end of the lane, with the fields stretching out in front of them. Al-Adawi turned to cast a glance behind him. He spotted Omran's shoulder sticking out from the entrance of one of the houses. He was standing on the stone bench; the entrance did not seem to be large enough to accommodate his vast body. Al-Adawi called out to him. Omran came out of his hiding place and walked up to them.

"Are you following me?" said al-Adawi.

"Following you?"

A Weak Light Revealing Nothing

They exchanged glances in silence. Al-Adawi was angry and his body leaned slightly backward, with his hands in the openings of his gallabia. Omran smiled as he looked around him.

"You're following me!" roared al-Adawi.

The penetrating smell. Omran raised his head, sniffing the air around him. With a fleeting glance he took in the packet and his eyes assumed a faraway look.

Al-Adawi drew his wife away and they moved off. Omran followed them with deliberate steps. Al-Adawi stopped and turned round to him.

"Go back, Omran!"

He stood, relaxed, looking at the two of them, and when al-Adawi and his wife moved off, he also moved.

Al-Adawi stopped, turning to his wife.

"What's up with him?"

He left her and walked up to him.

"Just let me look at it in the tin," said Omran, "and then I'll go off." He put out his hand for the packet and al-Adawi pushed it away.

"That's how it is. I'll give you some of what I've got in my pocket."

Omran's eyes gleamed for a brief moment, then he dashed toward al-Adawi and pressed him up against the wall. He struck at the package with his hand, making it fall. He was roaring, with his arm at al-Adawi's chest as he leaned against him with all his weight. Al-Adawi's wife screamed and began looking about her for a stone. Once again he pressed against him violently. He was breathing heavily and scowled at the woman as she approached. Then, suddenly, he left him and moved off.

Al-Adawi sank down against the wall. He was collecting his breath with difficulty. The woman took up the packet and helped him to his feet, and they went off to the fields.

❖

The river bank was packed with villagers. Some of them had climbed right up to the tops of the trees, though they saw

A Weak Light Revealing Nothing

nothing but the cannon crouching there. The two soldiers on their horses were blocking the road: no one could leave or enter the village. They had certainly stopped all trains and cars from both directions, for we saw none passing.

First of all, the fishermen emerged. They walked without looking around them. They passed between the two horses, and when we gathered around them, they pushed us off and continued on their way. Then we heard them shouting. They were over on a side road, where they were fighting, with the dust stirred up thickly around them. They grappled with each other, rolling about for a long time on the ground. Then the dust settled and each took up his basket and his net and went on his way.

A little after this Owais came out. He stood beside the cannon and felt around its muzzle, then he approached us. He was laughing and brushing down his gallabia.

"Where have they gone?" he shouted.

"Who?"

"The fishermen. They all received a hefty slap on the back of the neck . . . ," and he broke into laughter. "They were running like rats between the trees."

He looked at us as he sucked at the ends of his mustache.

"They asked them, 'Are you fishing?' They said, 'We're fishermen.' And they asked them, 'Where's the lake?' They said, 'Here.' And they asked them, 'How far away is it?'

"They looked at each other and didn't answer. The rags they were wearing were short and didn't hide anything. They were looking at the daylight that was beginning to come through the branches of the trees. They were thinking they would reach their homes under cover of the darkness of dawn, like other days.

"And they asked them, 'And do you always walk about like this?' And the fishermen bent down and looked at where they were pointing, and saw their private parts. They looked at each other and didn't say anything. 'Who do you think we are?' But the fishermen still didn't answer.

A Weak Light Revealing Nothing

"'Haven't you heard of the revolution?'
"They kept silent. Nothing on their faces showed they'd ever heard of it. Their chief was sitting on a chair, with another chair beside him. I thought to myself that those two chairs were strange—not like any of the village chairs. Do they carry them with them all the time? The chief was looking at me. When the fishermen had left, after getting only what they deserved, he beckoned me closer. He said, 'Do you want to sit down?' I said, 'God forbid that I should sit down in your presence.' He asked me the name of the village and I told him. And he asked me how far the lake was and I told him. I waited for him to ask me about the revolution, but he didn't ask. Then they let me go."

The sun glowed and the heat grew intense. The two soldiers were on their horses with the sweat moistening their faces. The horses stretched out their heads and began sniffing each other.

Trays of food made their appearance, on their way to the bridge. First of all the headman's tray came, giving off the aroma of rounds of freshly-baked bread and roast chicken; it was carried by a woman who had penetrated through the crowd of villagers at the head of the bridge and had come to a stop in front of the two soldiers. The headman, too, stopped alongside her, a clean scarf wrapped round his shoulders. One of the soldiers dashed off on his horse into the trees. He was away for a while, then returned. Taking up his previous position, he motioned to the woman to move away. The headman looked around him, then advanced hesitatingly. He did not advance very far because the soldier signaled him to stop. The other trays of food clustered behind the headman's tray, their owners standing alongside the women. The headman dried his sweat with the end of his scarf; he looked for a while at the two soldiers, who had become rigid on their horses, then he turned and went back. The trays turned round behind him and had hardly moved away from the approach to the bridge than hands were stretched to seize their contents.

A Weak Light Revealing Nothing

When some time had passed and nothing had happened, the villagers began to sneak off. Some of us remained on the bank. It was easy, once the crowd had thinned, to find comfortable places to sit.

"What are they doing over there?"

At last the sun had gone down and darkness had fallen. Faint lights moved between the trees as though people were carrying small lamps. Then they were put out, though one of them stayed on: it was hanging on the branch of a tree, its weak light revealing nothing. However, we were able to catch sight of a specter passing beside it from time to time. We stretched out on the ground, with our eyes on the light.

They were still over there when we got up later in the night after a nap and went home. The two soldiers were in the same position, just as we had seen them during the day, still blocking the bridge, while the darkness had lessened slightly with the approach of dawn.

By morning they had taken themselves off.

The Bend of the River

The tall eucalyptus trees grew more thickly at the bend of the river than those strung out along the bank. The shady patch was always damp, the earth looking as though it had been watered, covered with dried leaves. It was there that the boundaries of the village began. The villagers, on reaching it when returning home, would collect their breath and glance with loving reassurance at the tall trees. The donkeys would breathe heavily, shake their ears, and quicken their pace. The fishermen on their way back at noon from the lake would throw themselves down in the shade after the long distance they had come, and there they would divide up the fish and wash them in the waters of the river, ridding them of all traces of salt. Then they would put on their gallabias and go off to the market.

In summer the women of the big houses would come out of an evening for a short stroll. They would be in groups in their black *milaya* wrap-arounds, hiding their faces inside them and leaving nothing but a small opening in front of their eyes. They exuded a pleasant smell that distinguished them from the women of the other houses.

Their stroll would take them no further than the trees, where they would stand in the darkness, their milayas having fallen down to their shoulders. Then, with raised voices, they would break into a run, their laughter ringing among the trees. When a particularly loud burst of laughter rang out it would be followed by a sudden silence, and hands would be stretched out to settle the milaya on the shoulder, where

The Bend of the River

it would remain rather than being raised over the head. Their eyes would stare with curiosity through the trees as the moments passed. Then one of them would begin singing in a low voice and they would whisper to her to keep quiet. She would nevertheless continue with her singing, her voice rising little by little. Then they would go back to running about and laughing.

Usually the boys would be sitting on the bridge at the bend of the river. Those who had entered university and had come to spend the vacation in the village would sleep away the mornings at home, coming out in the afternoons, wearing trousers and shirts, their hair smarmed in brilliantine. After they had made their outing along the dirt road, they would begin talking in earnest, waving their arms about with raised voices. They would move backward and forward with graceful gestures, standing with one leg bent and a hand at the waist or behind the back, their faces aglow in the setting sun.

When the women reached the trees, the boys would appear not to notice their arrival, though a tinge of excitement would color their conversation. They would also be following, out of the corner of their eyes, the movement taking place among the trees and would catch sight of the milayas as they were waved about in the air and continue with their conversation. When laughter echoed among the trees, they would all of a sudden stop talking and listen intently. It would be for only a brief moment, after which they would go on with their conversation, which had begun to be listless, interspersed with periods of silence. Then they would seat themselves on the railing of the bridge and stare in silence toward the trees, as darkness had commenced to obscure the shape of things, the tops of the trees taking on the hue of the darkening clouds. They were nonetheless following the voices and laughter as they saw shadows running and darting between the trees.

Sometimes a young girl who had been accompanying the women would emerge from the clump of trees, and it would

The Bend of the River

seem as if the bridge had suddenly attracted her attention, for she would walk straight to it, wearing a clean dress and shoes, in her hair a knot of brightly-colored cloth. The boys on the railing would give the appearance of sharing in something slightly disturbing, as their eyes were fixed on the young girl coming up the road. She would stop for a moment in front of them, staring at them one by one. They would be riveted to their places, and then she would continue on to the end of the bridge. On her way back she would break into a run, paying them no attention, and their eyes would follow her until she had disappeared among the trees, after which they would once again sit back and relaxed.

When the moon was shining, the boys would catch sight of bare arms—which they always imagined as white and plump—waving about from time to time. They would see the women swaying with suppressed laughter, their milayas gathered about their waists, then walking along by the trees and coming to a stop where they ended, looking at the dark horizon, their milayas having worked loose and lying along their arms. A few scattered lights came into view and disappeared far off where the houses of the neighboring village lay. The silences between them would grow longer, then they would make their way back, their voices a whisper, their footsteps slow. They walked with their arms round each other's shoulders until they emerged from the trees. The village, now within sight, looked as they always saw it: dogs barked loudly; women and men—with children around them—were still seated in the darkness in front of their houses. Once again the milayas would be drawn about them, hiding their faces, as they stood for a while at the entrance to the village and then dispersed into the lanes.

The Girl Washes

The girl placed her bundle of clothes under her arm and went out onto the road.

The dawn haze was showing on the horizon and a thick white vapor crouched over the trees and the roofs of the closed houses. The earth was warmly wet, and under the trees the ground was very moist, with water still dripping from the leaves.

From the patch of vegetation the rats were leaping and scurrying along the road, then suddenly hurling themselves, in a great leap, to the other side, where the trees spread along the edge of the narrow irrigation canal. The road came to an end at the river.

The girl walked along the bank. The waters looked dark in the semi-blackness, and gleams of faint light suddenly came and went. Waves of white mist rose up far away from the water's surface. The other bank remained hidden amid thick clouds from which protruded the tops of eucalyptus trees. The girl came to a stop at the prayer-area. Pieces of white rock were rolling down into the river. She placed her clothes on a rock close to the water and took from them a piece of soap and a small roll of straw. Loosening the pigtails of hair, she slipped down into the water in her clothes. She immersed herself and rubbed her eyes, then drew near to the bank and removed her clothes.

A man who had been lying down in the prayer-room stirred, hiding behind the branch of a tree that slanted over it. His gallabia was dark, the color of the mud walls of the

The Girl Washes

prayer-area that stretched along beside him. His hand stealthily stretched out and moved aside the leaves between two small branches. His movement was so quiet that the little bird cowering under a broad leaf on one of the branches remained sitting there without stirring.

The girl placed her wet clothes on the white rock that broke the water's surface and rubbed the soap over them.

Her body was hidden beneath the water. She began beating the clothes with swift blows against the white rock, then got up, resting herself on her knees, and pressed down on her clothes with all her weight.

The water reached her middle; her body, when she bent down, gave the appearance of being intensely thin, the bones of her back projecting and her breasts small and quivering slightly.

She rinsed the clothes, squeezed them and bundled them up on the rock, while she seated herself on another rock and rubbed her body with the roll of straw and soap. The lather was thick on her head and face. Jumping into the water, she swam the width of the river, disappearing into the thick mist. She touched the other bank and then came back, followed by a slight cloud of mist.

She stood close to the bank. The water was covering her chest. She raised her breasts that undulated under the water. She plunged down for a while, then rose, and she saw them growing larger, then smaller. Supporting them on the palms of her hands, she moved against the current. The water was exerting a slight pressure, and she shivered a little, her face glowing.

Rays of light burst forth suddenly, piercing the layers of mist in a slanting line, while light was scattered on the surface of the river. The light was turbid, dull; it seemed to move with the current. The girl shrank back under the water and began to make her way to the bank.

The mist, surrounded by rays of light like remnants of wispy smoke, began to undulate as it moved away. Quickly

The Girl Washes

forming itself into thick masses, it softly flowed toward the light.

The girl squeezed her locks of hair. Bending over the white rock, she put on her dry clothes and, folding the wet ones under her arm, went up to the road.

Death Has its Time

It seemed that the people of the lane knew that the daughter of al-Dugheidi the head nightwatchman would be killed that night. From early morning there were only a few people walking in the lane, and those who happened to be passing through would quicken their pace as they approached the closed house. The shutters of the houses opposite were open and faces pressed behind the windows from time and then disappeared.

The house consisted of a single story in the middle of the lane; its large barred windows had been closed for two days. Its walled roof had long washing-lines stretched across it on which al-Dugheidi's wife's blue gallabia hung, the gallabia she wore when going to market.

At the corner of the lane was the shop of Khalil the grocer. He says he was the first to know. He hadn't said this openly but had whispered it to his wife, who had locked up the house, put on her headscarf, and followed him to the shop.

Unusually for him he had stayed awake the night before until a late hour. When the kerosene in the pressure-lamp had run out he had refilled it. His wife had been struggling against sleep inside the shop, where she had curled up in a corner among the empty crates and cartons. When the sound of her snoring grew too loud, he would remonstrate in a low voice. Since he had told her what he had seen she had been following him like his shadow. For the past two days she had been radiant and full of movement, turning round at every sound he made. Full of energy, she would go to the house and

Death Has its Time

come back with food. He would sit inside the shop, while she would look after the customers, asking him about prices and weights. He would gaze at her, enjoying seeing her move about inside the shop.

Every time the door to al-Dugheidi's house creaked, Khalil would peep out, with his wife behind him. He would feel as if the land was holding its breath, and the youngest of al-Dugheidi's sons, so tiny he could scarcely be seen, would go out, closing the door behind him. He would stand for a moment at the threshold rubbing his eyes, with the remnants of the straw from where he had been sleeping clinging to his hair. He would then rush to the shop and buy tobacco and cheese and tins of sardine. Khalil would stare into the boy's face, who each time gave the appearance of being asleep.

"All day the boy's not come."

"Maybe yesterday he took enough."

"Not at all. He took a single packet of cigarettes. Al-Dugheidi himself smokes three a day."

Two days ago Khalil had been standing sprinkling water in front of the shop. It was afternoon, the weather still hot. The shadows had begun to lengthen, covering the small open space in front of the shop. He had seen al-Dugheidi's daughter coming from the lane to the open space. She was wearing her mother's black shawl round her shoulders. Her breasts protruded and had grown fuller. The shawl hung down, hiding the opening in her dress. Like her mother, she would from time to time arrange the shawl, which was tied under her chin.

"How old is she?"

"There's exactly a week between her and my son Selim."

"Fourteen."

Up until recently she used to go out with the boys to the fields, returning in the afternoon with a bundle of grass for their donkey and the dark traces of mulberry round her mouth.

In the afternoon the boys would set up their soccer pitch on the edge of the open space and Khalil would see her

Death Has its Time

among them, imitating the women in the lane, with the boys around her exploding with laughter. Even from where he stood he could guess who the woman was she was imitating. One day he saw her imitating the way *he* walked.

She made her way to the shop, the boys behind her calling out, "Uncle Khalil . . . Uncle Khalil."

Her face was alight with suppressed laughter. He went out to the them and the boys scattered far and wide, while she stayed on looking at him.

One day at sunset she was dancing in the middle of a circle of boys, with a rope made of straw round her waist, wild flowers covering her head, and a pigtail of hair falling down onto her breast. Her father, who was returning home, saw her, and from that day she disappeared into the house.

Her voice trilled away the whole day inside and she would call out at the boys from the roof. Sometimes she would wear wooden clogs and stand at the partly open door and indicate to the girls in the lane that they should play in front of the door. She would crane out with half her body to rearrange the house they were fashioning, and when she spotted a stranger in the lane, she would hide behind the door, one side of her face showing, with her small nose and bulky pigtail.

It was afternoon, and she was standing at the edge of the open space. The boys were playing soccer and Khalil was shouting at them to go away. He saw her concealing her laughter in her shawl, with the boys scrambling violently around the ball amid dense dust. She began to cross the open space to the shop when her brother Abd al-Salam appeared, coming from the other side. He saw his sister and continued on his way to the house. The boys stopped playing and, striking the end of his gallabia with the cane, he passed between them, smiling. He was still proud about having come out of prison; wearing a well-ironed gallabia and polished shoes, he would stroll around the station and the coffee houses of the village. He was one of four in the village

Death Has its Time

of whose manliness the boys would boast. From time to time he would spend a month or three in prison after some fight he'd had. On the last occasion he had spent a whole year inside when he had been caught in the market selling a stolen animal. His father, too, was proud of him, taking him with him wherever he went. On market days the two of them would walk along side by side, with his other two sons, Shakir and Zeydan, behind them and his youngest boy holding the hand of one of them. They would take a long stroll, al-Dugheidi raising the end of his gallabia; the sweat poured down onto his plump face as he made his greeting in a booming voice. Often he would complete his outing without making any purchase.

The ball was with a boy standing at the top of the lane. As though wishing to show off his skill in front of Abd al-Salam, he gave the ball a hard kick. From the ball's flight Abd al-Salam guessed that it was going in the direction of his sister. He turned, as did Khalil, in warning. The girl bent down slightly and put her hands around her stomach, leaving her frightened face exposed to the ball which lightly touched her on the shoulder. Khalil spun round, hurling curses at the boys. He spotted the scowling face of Abd al-Salam: he was staring at his sister, who had adjusted her shawl and gone off to the shop. Khalil, perceiving what had happened, glanced at the girl's stomach.

"It wouldn't have meant anything if I hadn't seen her hands over her stomach. She looked like she was imitating a woman in her ninth month, but her face this time said she was not joking."

Abd al-Salam went up to her. The boys were frightened of him and retreated to the fringes of the open square. The girl came to a stop as though she sensed him behind her. When he was a couple of steps away, he called her in a low voice. He turned and made for the house, the girl walking behind him. She stood for a while in front of the threshold, looking all around her; then she entered, and he locked the door.

Death Has its Time

"It remained locked until sunset."

The youngest of al-Dugheidi's sons went out. He disappeared for a while, then returned with his father. Al-Dugheidi passed by the shop, then returned to it. The darkness of evening was advancing on the open space. He stood in front of the stone bench of the shop and belched. He asked for a packet of cigarettes. He looked hard at the coins in the semi-darkness. Saying something about the sons of bitches in the café, he laughed, then walked over to the house.

❖

Khalil was late locking up the shop. The street was empty and its whole length looked dark, the houses having put out their lights. The boys lay about all in a heap in the light of the pressure-lamp in front of the stone bench. When the lamp hanging from the ceiling was taken down, they awoke from their dozing and helped him lock up the shop. They walked off behind him, then began slinking away one after the other into the nearby lane.

On his way he passed by al-Dugheidi's house. The light coming from under the door was faint and he heard no sound. In the light of the pressure-lamp he saw the lengths of palm branches the girl had from time to time fixed to the side of the door.

"It's against envy, Uncle Khalil." And she gave a laugh, concealing it within her shawl. He used to laugh whenever he saw her in the black *milaya*, gesticulating with her hands as the women did.

He placed the pressure-lamp in the courtyard. He washed his face while his wife was preparing supper. He related to her what had happened, and laughed away his suspicions that had taken wings. His wife put out the kerosene stove and silence took over. The steam from the soup rose into her face as she emptied the cooking pot into the tureen.

She said that the girl was indeed pregnant and was in her fourth month.

Khalil brushed off the drops of water from his arms.

Death Has its Time

"A month ago her mother took her to Saadiya the midwife."

She took a small mouthful of soup, then squeezed half a lemon into it.

"And Saadiya refused. She said it was the fourth month. She was frightened. Three times she brought the girl to her. The last time Saadiya shut the door in her face."

"And who would it be?"

"No one knows, and Saadiya doesn't believe the story. The girl says it's a boy from the settlements. Some months ago she went with the boys to gather mulberries. The boys went ahead of her. She was up in a tree and the boy passed by and saw her. He climbed up to her."

"From which settlement?"

"The girl doesn't know. He filled her lap with mulberries for her."

❖

In the morning Khalil had his breakfast at the shop. It was early and the ground of the open space was still moist with dew. He saw al-Dugheidi's two sons, Shakir and Zeydan, crossing the open space, coming from the settlements. They were mounted on their donkeys, wrapped round in their cloaks, going along side by side. They came to a stop in front of the house, and each tied his donkey to the window. Then they entered and closed the door.

They are now among the best known carpenters in the settlements for making water-wheels; they work and live together in a single house over there. When they come to the village market, they come together, always dressed in the same cloth, a brown shawl wrapped round their heads.

When they left their father's house last year, they left it together. They had suddenly made the decision not to give their father a single millieme from then on. And because they knew what would happen, they had thought it best to have their confrontation with their father at the house, far from their new abode. On the day agreed they had returned early to the

Death Has its Time

house, taking with them a donkey-cart which they left a short distance away. They gathered together their tools and bits of wood, and they also took their clothes, some of which were still wet and hanging on the clothes-line. They made up two bundles by the front door, then stood in front of their father, who was sitting in the courtyard smoking and drinking tea. Al-Dugheidi listened to them in silence as he stared into their faces. He remained silent as, with the tip of his finger, he arranged the fire in the bowl of the water-pipe. The two exchanged glances, then turned to the door. Al-Dugheidi peered out from the courtyard and saw that water was dripping from the bundles; he followed the two of them with his eyes until they were outside. When he saw the donkey-cart he burst into a rage. Darting forward with a roar, he struck out at them. They remained silent before his blows. Then, overcome by a strong fit of coughing, he supported himself against the cart. The sons shook out their gallabias and put them on, then collected their scattered belongings. Perhaps thinking that the matter was at an end, al-Dugheidi yielded to them when they took hold of him under the arms and sat him down on the threshold. Then they got up into the cart and left the lane.

"I haven't see them since the last Feast," said Khalil.
"And who told them?" said his wife.

❖

Khalil was seated dozing in his chair on the stone bench, while his wife was inside the shop collecting up the empty crates and cartons and putting them in the yard. The light from the pressure-lamp had begun to dim and the boys huddled up beside the stone bench were fast asleep. The intensity of the heat had eased somewhat with the coming of night and there was a slight breeze.

Khalil woke to the sound of the creaking of the door and saw al-Dugheidi and his three sons standing in front of the house. One of the sons held the donkey's head, while the other two placed the load on its back. Then they looked in the direction of the shop.

Death Has its Time

"Turn off the lamp," whispered Khalil.

He carried his chair inside and half closed the double door to the shop. He saw the donkey approaching, with the youngest of the sons riding it; there was a tied sack in front of him. He crossed the open space and disappeared into a side street that led to the river.

The three men were still standing there. One of them coughed, then they entered the house.

The Floating Sack

Close to dawn Darwish the maker of drums leaves home and makes for the lock-gate, his wife behind him carrying the lamp on her head. This is normally on the days when the gate that joins the canal to the river is closed, and the bodies of animals float in the sluice in front of it amid foam, garbage, and weeds.

Darwish stands on the bank staring into the middle of the sluice, seeing nothing in the darkness. He has, however, seen the bodies of dead animals during the daytime. Mumbling some invocations, he goes down to the bank, while his wife sits on a stone slab (which she placed there years ago), her back against the trunk of a tree.

Darwish removes his clothes and throws them to his wife, who puts them in a heap on her lap. He leans over, hiding his genitals with both hands, and slips into the sluice, plunging down into the dingy waters that push him to the gate. He is conscious of the touch of the cold iron and of the smell of rust diffused sharply amid the smells of dead animals and garbage. The sound of the waters echoes deeply behind the gate. He circles the corpse, feels it with both hands and murmurs, "A water buffalo."

And his wife is on the bank. She has bent over slightly and extended her hand with the lamp as she waits for his trembling whisper. At this moment she feels the tremor and, drawing her legs together, throws him the end of the rope, which he grasps in his teeth. He plunges under the body, tying the rope round it, then he pushes it to the bank and his

The Floating Sack

wife draws on the rope until the two of them bring it out of the water. Darwish places a rag around his middle and begins to skin the body, while his wife hovers above his head with the lamp, as the light of dawn begins to gleam on the horizon.

It is he alone who comes across the corpses of pregnant young girls that the river sweeps along on its way, casting them up with other bodies at the sluice in front of the gate. This generally happens in the days when the maize stalks have become tall and Darwish gazes at them suspiciously. He sits of an afternoon at the threshold of his house and notices the tassels of the maize stalks leaning over with the wind—and he spits and lets out a curse. And at night when the moon is shining and he sees them standing straight, having abandoned themselves to stillness, there issues from them a soft rustling sound, and the croaking of frogs rises up rhythmically, and small animals scurry about, then disappear into them soundlessly.

One day his wife said to him, "Why the maize patches?"

"How should I know?"

He fell silent and his eyes explored the maize patch in front of his house.

Every time he plunges into the sluice, he flexes his legs, never stretching them out, and circles round the body of the water buffalo, keeping his feet away from the depths of the water; nevertheless he feels the closed sack as though it were attached to his feet.

"They never float—it's as though they're waiting for me."

He turns around, leaving the body of the water-buffalo, and plunges his arm down to feel the end of the sack: the human head and the two feet. He pushes the sack to the bank.

His wife feels the rope growing slack in her hand. She leaves the lamp on the slab and hurries to him.

"Hang on to it, woman."

The two of them raise the sack between them to the bank. Darwish's wife looks as though a sense of alertness has

The Floating Sack

pervaded her all of a sudden. She circles round the sack with the lamp, her gallabia drawn up over her legs.

"Let me see her," she calls out. "Let me see her—she's from the village. By the Prophet, she's from our village."

Suddenly she leans over the sack and tears it apart where the head of the corpse is.

Darwish hurries off to put on his gallabia, for he cannot bear to stand naked in front of the corpse of a woman. But when his wife cries out he turns round and throws a stone at her, so she jumps away, then she returns with a stick in her hand to pull the sack away from the corpse's face. Darwish chases after her waving the rope, so, protesting volubly, she hastens up to the road. Darwish wheels round in search of someone to send to the headman. Dawn, though, is still on the horizon. He looks at his wife anxiously, then sends her to the headman's house.

Darwish stands on the road, tall, exceedingly thin, with his neck stretched out like a goose, listening for some sound. At such moments he has the sensation of someone there watching him. He walks a little, then returns, and stands without moving, his neck thrust out. Suddenly he perceives that the corpse's face is protruding, bloated, from the hole in the sack made by his wife. He descends to the bank hurriedly and covers the face with one of the rags his wife always has with her. Once again he stands on the road. The darkness of dawn has begun to soften and red coloring glows on the horizon.

Sometimes he catches sight of the man with the watching eyes lying down in the prayer-area close by, his head looking out over the low wall, and Darwish gives the impression of having seen nothing, his head lowered, looking away from the corpse.

Generally the one with the watching eyes has walked a long way, then lain down, waiting to be near at the final moments. He is one of her relatives, whom they have sent after throwing her corpse into the river. He has waited for a

The Floating Sack

day, then followed the sack. He walks along the bank. The corpse, however, is still at the bottom, being rolled about gently by the flow of water. He sees it sometimes as it becomes attached to the root of a tree on the bank, so he pushes it with his stick so that it again plunges down into the water.

He stays away from the bank for another day, then returns and stares down into the waters. It seems as if he has lost all trace of the sack, and his feet lead him to the neighboring village. He spends the evening at the café, huddled up on a chair in a dark corner, his long stick between his legs and a broad, dark-colored shawl wound round his head and half his face.

When the café closes, he moves to the mosque to spend the night, and in the morning he again searches the river bank.

Suddenly the corpse floats to the surface. Generally this happens on the third day, when he sees it slightly ahead of him. At other times he sees it approaching from afar. The sack looks stationary, as though sticking to the surface, dragging behind it weeds and garbage it has brought up from the bottom.

It twists slightly to float crosswise. The waters round it are agitated and impede its movement. The front sinks down and the water scatters over it, sparkling. Then it rights itself, moving into the middle of the river's flow, and it rocks slightly, as though shaking off the fine spray of water, and continues on its way.

The men about to pray regard it as they are making their ablutions in the river, and interrupt their ablutions to mutter invocations. Their movements on the concrete steps are stilled as they lower their eyes until it draws away.

The sack seems to have begun to dawdle in its push forward. Raising their heads, they find it still there in front of them; once again they recite invocations, their voices slightly raised.

The sack sways gently, turning round on itself, its front toward them, the extended shadows of the trees dancing

The Floating Sack

above it. There are eddies in front of the steps of the mosque, and it looks as if it will never emerge from them. Then, in a moment, it is pushing forward and drawing away, continuing on its journey.

The women are on the bank, their belongings scattered about them. One of them spots the floating sack and lets out a low cry as her hand strikes her breast. The outlines of the corpse are delineated through the exposed part of the sack: the extended stomach, the slope of the thighs, the roundness of the breasts, and the hair that flows out from between the narrow threads of the sack.

The women cling together as silence settles over them, and when it seems that the currents have begun to shift the sack in the direction of the bank, they dart into the river and beat the surface of the water with the clothes they have washed, shouting loudly. The successive circles created by their blows widen. The sack rocks slightly and continues on its way.

When it leaves the boundaries of the village, the man with the watching eyes suddenly makes his appearance on the bank with his stick, walking not far away. Pushing back the shawl from his head, he takes out a packet of food from his pocket and eats. Sometimes he rests in the shade of a tree, dozing with his eyes fixed on the sack as it draws away, after which he lengthens his stride to catch it up.

The crows hover and disappear between the branches of the trees, then again hover and circle above the sack noiselessly. The man picks up stones and walks alongside the sack, having wrapped the shawl around his head.

Suddenly the crows swoop, darting down and folding their wings above the sack. The man shouts, waves his shawl, and throws pieces of rock at them when they alight in the trees. He continues chasing them until they make off.

Sometimes the sack becomes stuck in the reed canes and weeds on the other bank and the current seems to be making it stick tighter.

The Floating Sack

The man comes and goes. He sees no dikes within sight. When the pathway is empty of passers-by, he takes off his clothes and slips into the water, carrying his stick. He comes to a stop close to the sack and pushes it with the stick until he frees it from the reed canes. The sack slues violently, then rights itself and continues on its way.

Finally it is free of the weeds and garbage that were clinging to it, and the water—after it has left the village—has become clean and glowing, surging and striking at it lightly. The bank here is bare of trees. It approaches the sluice in front of the lock and the man sees it submerge with lightning speed; the gate being shut, it circles round twice then disappears amid the bodies of animals that are there.

The man sees that it is sufficiently far away from the village; he brushes down his shawl, winds it round his head, and returns to the village. Near dawn, when feet tread in the mosque courtyard, he is taking up his stick and leaving.

Sometimes days pass without Darwish going near the lock. He is lying down at home when he hears a rap at the window and sees the dawn light filling the courtyard of the house, and he opens the door and hears a whispering. "The lock."

He sees a man standing against the wall, his shawl wound round his head and face and his long stick alongside him.

"Right away," Darwish whispers.

The man stretches his hand to his pocket and Darwish, moving away, whispers, "God forbid."

"A sheet."

"I'll bring it."

And the man vanishes.

Darwish goes out, an old sheet under his arm, followed by his wife, who is looking around her.

"Don't look," Darwish whispers.

Once on the road he sends her to the headman's house, while he goes off to the lock. He slides down into the sluice with his gallabia on and pushes the sack to the bank, covering

The Floating Sack

it over with the sheet, then stands on the road, ringing out the ends of his gallabia, which is sticking to his body.

The headman appears on the road with the start of the day. Behind him are Darwish's wife and a throng of men, women, and children who were on their way to the fields. Seeing the headman muttering to himself angrily in the lanes, they followed him.

"God damn you, Darwish, and curse your black days!" shouts the headman as he sets eyes on Darwish.

Darwish spots the end of the long stick amid the crowd of villagers, and sees them make way for the animal-drawn cart. They gently place the sack on it, while his wife pulls away the sheet from on top of it, and Darwish scolds her hotly. At that moment he feels the eyes of the man with the stick watching him. He does not turn to him, however. Then, later, he sees him as he turns and walks away along the road.

A Conversation at Night

There is a dim light in the café. The man sitting there in the semi-dark corner turned round. He gazed at me for a moment then continued looking at the empty tables. He looked at me again. He took a last sip from the glass of tea and took up a suitcase from beside him. He was old, very thin, and had a heavy gait. He passed by me to the open door and stood there. The streets were quiet and almost empty of passers-by. The rain had not come to a complete stop and there was still a light drizzle.

From the window I was watching the vendor of sausage sandwiches in front of the cinema and the steam that rose from the grilled meat behind the glass of his small cart. From time to time he would stretch out his head from behind the cart and signal that he would be coming right away.

At the door the old man said, "At night people go off to their homes."

Turning round, he approached. He looked at the things scattered on the table.

"Do you carry them all about with you? A strip of pills. Ah, I recognize them: indigestion tablets. I recognize those too: they're for colonic convulsions. One pill half an hour before meals. And a lighter. Chewing gum. A key-chain. A toothpick: do you use them? Better than a matchstick. Have you ever seen a thief?"

"Often."

He sat down, placing the suitcase on a chair beside him. Despite the two locks on either side he had tied round its

A Conversation at Night

middle a piece of thin string. He said, laughing, "I became aware of him after he'd taken the wallet from my pocket. I was on my way to the clinic and was standing in the crowd at the top of the street for the procession to come to an end. The open car and the President, with others with him. I was watching the procession and looking closely so I could tell the children about it on my return. No sooner do you lose something than you become aware of it. I spotted it in his hand before he hid it in his coat pocket. He was making his way through the crowd for the pavement. I shouted to him that it had no money in it. 'Here it is!'—and I waved three ten-pound notes. I told him I never put any money in the wallet."

From his coat pocket he took out a plastic wallet with a thin rubber band round it.

"No one would have been aware if he had gone on his way. But he turned round and hurled it at me, laughing, and the people around him laughed."

Unhurriedly he took off the rubber band. "People in Cairo are very nice. You won't find their like anywhere. Ah, what would I have done if he'd taken it? I can't move without it."

The vendor brought the plate of sandwiches. I thrust it toward the old man, who excused himself with a smile. "I'm not allowed them. I used to have them at noon and at night when I came to Cairo. He makes the best sausage sandwiches."

He dried both sides of his mouth, which was almost toothless.

"They stopped me from having all sorts of things. Now it's nothing but yogurt and boiled vegetables."

"The doctors?"

"Who else? They went over me from tip to toe." He laughed. "It doesn't seem as if you come here much."

"Very little."

"I come two or three times a month. The best thing about this café is that nothing in it changes. For twenty years. You go away and come back and find it as you left it."

A Conversation at Night

He placed the rubber band round his wrist and took out from the wallet some photos the size of playing cards. He tapped them into an arrangement on the table. He extracted from the inner pocket of his coat a picture wrapped round in paper. He wiped it with his handkerchief and added it to the other pictures.

"The last one—I had it taken today."

He placed his glasses on the end of his nose. "I don't think they'll be needing any more pictures after that."

He gazed at them one after the other and put them back in order. He was on the point of returning them to the wallet when he glanced at me hesitantly. Then he took one out and handed it to me. "A picture of sound waves. It's written on the back. You wouldn't believe it's the liver. Cirrhosis. Only a quarter is functioning. You've got it in the picture. I had it taken two years ago. And this one—the picture's taken by endoscopy. I don't know the esophagus from the duodenum. On the day I forgot to write on the back of them. I had them taken about a year and a half ago. The duodenum ulcer never gives me any pain. The pain is here in the side. It comes and goes. Perhaps it was the kidney. Look—the stone doesn't show up in it. If you'd only seen it in the X-ray—it was like a rock on the ocean bed." He laughed. "Branching off here and there. And this one"— he undid a folded piece of paper—"is merely a zigzag line. Electrocardiogram under stress. An obstruction of the coronary artery. The last one is of the spleen. Look how it's as blown up as a balloon. They say it's stopped functioning."

He retained some pictures in his hand. I handed him the ones I had. He collected them up together. He smoothed over the edges with his thumbs. I was thinking about what I could say. I saw him sunk in contemplation of them, the lineaments of his face having softened, his eyes looking like two firebrands that have come to life for a moment under the ashes.

"Like fingerprints—they're infallible."

He placed them in his wallet and wound the band round it.

A Conversation at Night

The drizzle was still falling. It was difficult to see it, though I could hear the sound of its monotonous rapping on the wet asphalt. I became conscious of the sound of his voice. He was relating something, then he asked me, "You don't come here much?"

"Very little."

"I know all the café's clients. They think I've gone away now. I got the suitcase ready, then the rain came down. And Hagg Sayyid, too. You don't know him?"

"Maybe I've seen him."

"He won't let me sleep in the hotel. He leaves me the couch." He pointed to a couch deep inside the café not far from the counter. The light there was out and the boy behind it was fast asleep.

"And the cold?"

"I never feel it. Hagg Sayyid leaves a fire in the brazier, and he keeps the two blankets in the small cupboard behind the pillar. He will be surprised when he comes in to close the café and sees me." He laughed. "Every morning he brings me breakfast: yogurt and cucumber. Do you see the picture over there?"

"Where?"

"On the building opposite?"

I hesitated. It seemed he was going to say something else. I was getting ready to leave. He had seen me gathering up my things from the top of the table. I looked to where he was pointing. The picture was rectangular, a meter long approximately. It was stuck to the wall, slightly above the ground.

"The Citadel?"

Saying this, I moved back the chair to get up. It seemed he hadn't noticed the move I'd made and was staring outside.

"I don't know. I haven't seen the Citadel. What d'you think is underneath it? Six pictures of the President, one on top of the other. How many years have passed? There were three boys, university students. They entered the café. They had a yellow cloth with them, which they spread out on the

A Conversation at Night

table, and some of those pens that are like brushes. They were writing. Hagg Sayyid saw them but didn't notice what they were doing. The same with me. I was sitting with him on the couch and I didn't notice what they were doing. Then there was the police raid—an officer, and men in plain clothes. It appears the boys were planning to go out into the streets with the cloth. You would have seen one of the boys fix the cloth to his back and run like a rocket amid the cars and the crowd. There would be a boy in front of him and another one behind. They would be running in silence, not shouting a single word. You weren't given the time to read what they'd written on the cloth. Suddenly the boy would come to a stop and turn around, as though to make us read. Then off he'd dart again. The cars would come to a stop, as did the people. Then you would see the plain-clothes men following after them. How they came to be there you wouldn't know—with the yellow overcoat on top of the gallabia and a stick under the arm—and sometimes with a black or gray sweater done up to the neck with a zip-fastener, and a newspaper held folded in the hand. I was with Hagg Sayyid on the couch and we turned round at the boys' shouts. They were dragging them outside. Hagg Sayyid and I approached and I spotted the word "Israel" before the officer folded up the cloth. I now remember it was at the same time as they announced "the visit of peace." Hagg Sayyid wanted to calm things down by saying something when he saw blood flowing from the nose of one of the boys. They took him along too. Oh yes, they took him." He laughed and took a toothpick that was still on the table. He placed the end between his lips.

"I waited here for him for two whole days and nights. He never said what happened to him. He no longer engages in conversation as he used to do. He just listens to you and says a word or two. I went away and came back more than once, and off people went to Israel, and he stayed just as he was."

He laughed and sucked at his hollow cheeks. "What happened after that I didn't see. Hagg Sayyid told me about it later

A Conversation at Night

on. When he heard of a demonstration being held, he used to stay on, lurking in the café until everyone had gone out. And after the lights were put out and the door was drawn to and half closed, he would go out with the mug and the brush. He would cross the street to the pavement opposite. The picture is there under that of the Citadel. One stroke of black with the brush aimed at the smiling face and he comes back. Hardly a day passes without his finding a new picture has been stuck over the previous one. He moves only when demonstrations break out. Only once he didn't wait for demonstrations. In the picture they had stuck up he was looking angry and was making a threatening gesture with his hand. He gave it two strokes with the brush. On other days he would sit in his corner on the couch smoking the water-pipe, paying no attention to the smiling face in the new picture. Twice, three times. Then he became aware of two faces he had not seen before coming regularly to the café. They would come immediately after the new picture had been stuck up. One of them would sit beside the window and after several days would disappear. On the last occasion the two of them came together. The smiling face, having received a stroke from the brush, was still on the wall. They searched the café inch by inch. He doesn't keep the mug and the brush in the café; he hides them among the rocks in the ruins behind the café. He would sneak out there from the back door. They took him with them and they turned me out, together with my suitcase, and locked up the café. In the morning they freed him. Why do you think they let him go?"

He was staring into my face, smiling. "Someone the same night painted over the smiling face with a brush. Ah." He laughed. "Hagg Sayyid was baffled. And after that they stuck up the picture of the Citadel . . ."

I placed the remainder of my things in my pocket and moved the chair back. He gazed at me, smiling. "Do you always carry them in your pocket?"

Before I rose to my feet, a small, slight man entered. He paid no attention to us. He went straight to the counter. I

A Conversation at Night

guessed he was the owner of the café. He hung his stick on the wall and took off his cloak. The old man beside me took up his suitcase and walked up to him. Life suddenly filled the far corner. The boy behind the counter put on the light, lit the fire in the brazier, and carried the water-pipe to them. The singing voice of Umm Kulthum rang out. The two of them were talking and laughing as I left.

The Prisoner

They brought him by night. His blurred figure looked tall in the darkness of the cell. We could hear his quiet movements as he prepared his bedding in the corner. He was suppressing his cough so as not to disturb us. Seated with his arms around his knees, he had leant his head against the wall; after a while he rested it on his knees that were drawn together.

Later he told us that he couldn't sleep lying down, for his coughing became so violent it rent his chest. In the morning I took him with me to receive his rations, and when we went out into the light I noticed how very thin he was. He walked with his head inclined to one side, as though listening closely to some faraway sound. His face was pale and his thin lips wet with saliva.

I asked him his name. He turned toward me warily, then said that there had been a mistake, that he had no connection with anything. He went on staring into my face with eyes that were watering from the light of the sun and which he wiped with the back of his hand.

I told myself that this was the first time for him, for they generally said that at the beginning.

We stood in the jostle of prisoners at the kitchen entrance. The thick steam was coming out and flowing over us in successive viscid waves. We pushed the crowd into the kitchen. Two of the prisoners, bare-chested, were standing on a stone bench emptying a sack full of lentils into the large black cauldron. Rats jumped out of the sack, giving a short leap before dropping down into the cauldron. With another

The Prisoner

swift jump they hovered, for a fleeting moment, amid the steam, their tails erect, then fell back into the cauldron. One of the prisoners standing on the bench stretched out his hand and picked one of them up. He called out, laughing, as he transferred it from hand to hand; then, seizing it by the tail, he shook it for a while in the steam and threw it into the cauldron.

The two prisoners, their chests sticky with the steam, circled round the large cauldron, each holding a long stick. Leaning against these with their shoulders, they would plunge the end into the cauldron. From time to time they would together let out a loud cry, then exchange glances, and stop, breathless, enveloped by thick waves of steam, while they stared at the prisoners blocking the entrance to the kitchen.

I noticed him as he began to shake alongside me, at the same moment bending over and grasping hold of my shoulder. I dragged him outside. Leaning against the wall, he brought up the contents of his stomach and curled up, gasping for breath. I left him and returned to the kitchen, where the two prisoners on the bench were stirring the lentils in the cauldron. The force of the steam had abated slightly and the sound of the glowing bubbles was muted amid the silence. They looked at each other and laughed and began slowly to move round the cauldron. Their chest muscles were twitching in unison. Then, standing side by side, they bent forward slightly, leaning on their sticks, and looked and laughed at the prisoners at the kitchen entrance. Drops of sweat slid down their sticky chests.

I became aware of him as he returned and stood beside me and took the dish from my hand. His face was pallid.

"It's my stomach," he whispered.

We were gazing toward the two prisoners on the bench. They were continuing with the strange movements they made every time we went in to receive our ration of food. The guard on his chair in the far corner, eating his breakfast, gave

The Prisoner

two taps with his stick on the table in front of him. The two prisoners did not seem to notice the tapping of the stick and continued in their movements, changing places without letting the sticks slip from under their arms. Then one of them withdrew his stick from the cauldron and licked at the lentils sticking to it, while the other raised a jerrycan of water from behind him and poured it into the cauldron. The two of them were flooded in waves of steam which soon cleared, and once again they came into view, standing together laughing soundlessly.

"D'you know," he whispered beside me, "I've got no spleen."

When I turned to him he nodded his head in affirmation, smiled, and indicated the side of his stomach.

"Years ago."

From where he sat the guard pointed his stick at us. We began retreating, pressing our backs against the crowd behind us. His stick continued pointing at us until we were outside the kitchen entrance. The two on the bench were circling around inside in the semi-darkness, with the blaze of the fire under the cauldron reflected on their bare chests. They were feeding it with pieces of wood that they picked up from a pile to the side as they circled around, with the spray of scalding lentils spattering onto them from the large bubbles. Then they began to slow down as they circled round, their arms dangling slackly, and to sing in a low murmur.

The guard rose to his feet and passed by them, then came back and rained down blows on them with his stick. The blows left red weals on their backs. They carried on with their slow pace and faint song, while the guard made off to the corner where the pitcher of water stood.

I felt him fall down beside me, his fingers digging into my shoulder. We carried him between us. His body was rigid. We placed him by the wall. His limbs were stretched out as they shook, and a strange sound, a harsh moaning, issued from his throat. I thrust his skull-cap between his teeth and

The Prisoner

brought his arms together on his chest, though once again they sprang apart. His mouth was twisted and his eyes bulged.

After a while his body relaxed and the moaning stopped. He felt the ground around him and gazed at me in astonishment. His face looked like that of a child about to drop off to sleep. I left him and returned to the kitchen. The two prisoners stood motionless by the heap of wood, staring into space through the kitchen entrance, while the guard stood on the bench, the ladle in his hand.

When I went back I found him still by the wall. He got to his feet and followed me.

The Condemned Man

I was on remand in prison awaiting sentence. The prison was like some small neglected railway station. The accused came for several days, then after sentence went off to other prisons.

In the morning they would take us out into the courtyard: there were cracks in the walls and the ceilings of some of the blocks were sagging, with twisted iron rods protruding; wooden beams had been placed in position to support them.

It was a narrow courtyard surrounded by a high wall with iron arches, between which was stretched barbed wire. It screened off all movement outside, though in the buildings around people would stand on the balconies and look at us.

Generally I would look about for some place in the sun, and I'd take off my blue coat and shake it free of insects.

I, who had been waiting longer than the others, would see new faces each morning. I would search for those I had come to know in the past few days and would find that they had disappeared. An intimate relationship would quickly spring up like a blazing fire and we would exchange secrets at a single sitting. After it we would separate and then disappear.

There were some among us who had been condemned to death and who were waiting for confirmation of the sentence. They would seem, in their red clothes, to be like tokens of danger among the other blue clothes.

For a few days I found there were two of them, then they became three. They, too, had waited longer than the others. And now that there were four of them, I would look about for them each morning. They would be gathering up the refuse

The Condemned Man

from the prison courtyard. Each of them would walk on one side of the courtyard dragging behind him an open-mouthed sack. We would make way for them in their tour. They would pick up leaves and cigarette ends, throw them into the mouths of the sacks, and move on. When two of them met up they would exchange a brief sideways look and each would glance at the other's sack and move away.

At noon each of them would choose some place far away from the others. He would seat himself with his back to the wall, his open sack beside him and the container of food in front of him. They would eat quickly; it seems to be the moment when they look around them. A slight astonishment shows in their eyes, which soon disappears; their faces grow wearily sullen and they sink into something resembling a daze, their heads tilted slightly backward. Then, suddenly, one of them rises to his feet, dragging his sack behind him. The others are aware of him and turn, watching him with heavy eyes. They also rise to their feet and go their separate ways in the courtyard.

In the afternoon we would go up to the cells, while they would stay on in the courtyard. I would see them through the small window walking far apart up to the end of the courtyard, then returning, dragging their sacks behind them. They would always find something to pick up, for, with the wind blowing, dry leaves never stopped falling, and sometimes sudden gusts would hurl pages of old newspapers and light garbage in from the street.

The shadow of the building extends to cover the open courtyard. The guards sit on their chairs beside the gate, and there is a guard with a rifle in the wooden sentry box on top of the wall. He advances two steps along the wooden base and stands for a moment with the sun flooding him, looking around him, then turns and goes back to the sentry box.

When the sun began to set they would drag their sacks to the gate, securely tie up the mouth, leave them at the feet of the guards to await the cart which would be coming from outside, and would go back into the building.

The Condemned Man

There were four of them, then they became three. I would awake to the faint noise that would accompany the execution of one of them at dawn, and would remain listening until it vanished. And now they have become two, walking in opposite directions. The sack of the one walking beside the wall would be fuller than the other's. They would, however, exchange places. This would be initiated by the man with the less full sack. On reaching the end of the courtyard he would move over to the side of the wall, while the other, dragging his sack, would take his place. They were, it seems, anxious that neither's sack should be filled more than the other's.

In the morning I saw him over there—just as I had imagined him when I heard the slight noise at dawn—standing alone in a corner of the courtyard under the sentry box, grasping the open end of the sack and looking at the prisoners in their blue clothes. They were gathered by the kitchen, where the smell of hot bread was diffused. He leaned his back against the wall, a cigarette in his mouth. Then, dragging his sack, he walked off unhurriedly. He passed by fallen leaves, cigarette ends, and the dead rats that the prisoners had thrown to the side of the wall. Halfway down the courtyard, he began to bend over and pick them up, throwing them into the opening of the sack.

A Conversation from the Third Floor

She came to the place for the second time. The policeman stared down at her from his horse.

It was afternoon. The yellow wall stretched right along the road. Inside the wall was a large rectangular three-story building; its small, identical windows looked more like dark apertures. The woman stood a few paces away from the horse. The policeman looked behind him at the windows, then at the woman. He placed both hands on the pommel of the saddle and closed his eyes. After a while the horse moved and came to a stop crossways in the street. Then, a moment later, it made a half-turn and once again stood at the top of the street.

The woman came two steps forward. The horse bent one of its forelegs, then gently lowered it.

"Sergeant, please, just let me say two words to him."

His eyes remained closed, his hands motionless on the pommel.

Above the wall stretched a fencing of barbed wire, at the end of which was a wooden tower. Inside there stood an armed soldier.

The woman took another step forward.

"You see, he's been transferred . . ."

The sun had passed beyond the central point in the sky, but the weather was still hot. A narrow patch of shade lay at the bottom of the wall.

The woman transferred the child to her shoulder.

A Conversation from the Third Floor

When she looked again at the policeman's face, she noticed two thin lines of sweat on his forehead.

Quietly she moved away from in front of the horse and walked beside the wall. About halfway along it she sat down on a heap of stones facing the building.

The prisoners' washing, hung by the arms and legs, could be seen outside the bars of the windows. Mostly it was completely motionless, even with the breeze that blew from time to time.

The woman whispered to herself, "They must be wet."

She placed the child in her lap. For a moment her eyes fastened on a gallabia that gently swayed to the movement of the wind. She stretched out her leg and gazed at her toes and the dried mud that clung to them. She rubbed her feet together, then gazed at them once again.

Putting back her head, she looked up at the windows of the third floor with half-closed eyes.

The soldier in the tower took a step forward. He rested his head against the edge of the wooden wall.

He looked at the sky, at the roofs of the houses, at the street, then at the head of the white horse.

Suddenly a shout broke the silence. The woman quickly drew back her leg. She caught sight of a bare arm waving from between the bars of a window on the third floor.

"Aziza! Aziza! It's Ashour."

She moved a step nearer to the wall and stared in silence at the window.

"It's Ashour, Aziza. Ashour."

She saw his other arm stretching out through the window. She searched with her eyes for something between the two arms and succeeded in making out a face pressed between the two bars. Other faces could be seen above and alongside him.

"Aziza, I've been transferred. Did you get my letter? In four days I'll be transferred. Did you prune the two date palms? Where are Hamid and Saniyya? Why didn't you bring them with you? I'm being transferred. Where's Hamid?"

A Conversation from the Third Floor

He turned round suddenly, shouting:
"Stop it, you bastards!"
She heard him shouting and saw the faces disappear from the window. After a while his face was again looking out through the bars, then the other faces looked out above his.
"Aziza!"
She looked at the policeman on the horse, then at the soldier in the tower.
"Who are you holding? Shakir? Aziza!" She shook her head twice.
"Lift him up. Lift him up high."
She took the child between her hands and lifted him above her head.
She noticed his arms suddenly being withdrawn inside and his hands gripping the iron bars of the window. Then his face disappeared from view. For a while she searched for him among the faces that looked down. She lowered her arms a little and heard shouts of laughter from the window. She spotted his arm once again stretching outwards, then his face appeared clearly in the middle.
"Up, Aziza. Up. Face him toward the sun so I can see him." She lowered her arms for a moment, then raised him up again, turning his face toward the sun. The child closed his eyes and burst out crying.
"He's crying."
He turned round, laughing.
"The boy's crying! The little so-and-so! Aziza, woman, keep him crying!"
He cupped his hand round his mouth and shouted, "Let him cry!"
Again he laughed. A few shouts went up around him. She heard their words and shoutings. Then she saw his large nose poking out through the bars.
"Woman! Don't be silly, that's enough! Cover the boy—he'll get sunstroke!"
She hugged the child to her chest and saw the soldier withdrawing inside the tower.

A Conversation from the Third Floor

"Did you prune the two date palms?"
She shook her head.
"Why not? Why don't you talk? I'm being transferred. Pass by Abu Ismail and tell him I send him my best wishes—he'll do it as a favor and prune the trees, then you can bring along a few dates. Did you bring the cigarettes?"
She made a sign with her hand.
"Talk. What are you saying?"
"You've got them."
"Louder, woman."
"You've got them, I sent them to you."
"When ?"
"Just now."
"Just now? Here, hang on—don't move."
He disappeared suddenly. Two faces remained at the window. One of them stretched out his arm; he made an obscene movement in the air with his hand. She lowered her eyes, then went back to the pile of stones.
"Aziza!"
Though she did not recognize the voice, she looked up at the window. She saw the man was smiling, his arm still moving about. The second man was kneeling, having raised his gallabia above his thighs. She heard him call out:
"Aziza, look!"
She smiled. The policeman was still sitting on his horse as though asleep. From the side window of the tower she had a partial view of the soldier's head. He had taken off his helmet.
She heard several voices calling her. She listened attentively, concentrating her gaze on the soldier's head as he moved within the opening of the window. The calls were repeated, interspersed with abuse. The soldier put on his helmet, but remained inside the tower.
Suddenly the voices were silent and some moments later the breathless voice of her husband came to her:
"Aziza? I said five—didn't I tell you five packets?" She stared up toward him in silence.

A Conversation from the Third Floor

"Woman, what's the use of three packets?" She gestured to him with her hand.

"What are you saying?"

"Five—I sent five."

"Five?" he shouted fiercely. "The bastards!"

He disappeared suddenly, then leant out again shouting: "Wait! Don't go!"

She turned her face toward the window of the tower. He was away for a while, then he returned.

"It's all right, Aziza. Never mind. Five—yes, there were five. Never mind, a couple got taken, it doesn't matter. Listen—what was I going to say?" Silence. She saw him staring out in silence from the window. She shook out her black gallabia and walked forward toward the wall. He smiled.

"Aziza, I was about to say something to you."

Again there was silence. She turned away her head so that part of her face was against the sun. She shifted her head-veil slightly from her head.

"They took a couple of packets. Never mind, Aziza. Never mind."

He laughed. His voice had become calm. The other faces disappeared from above him, only a single face remaining alongside his.

"Did you build the wall?"

"Not yet."

"Why not?"

"When Uncle Ahmed lights the furnace, I'll get some bricks from him."

"All right. Be careful on the tram. Look after the boy."

She remained standing.

"Anything you want?"

"No."

She gazed at his face, his large nose, his bare arms. She smiled. The face next to his smiled back.

Suddenly he shouted. "Did you get the letter? I'm being transferred."

"Where to?"

A Conversation from the Third Floor

"I don't know."
"When?"
"You see, they're pulling down the prison."
"Where will you go?"
"God knows—anywhere. No one knows."
"When?"
"In two or three days. Don't come here again. I'll let you know when I'm transferred. Has the boy gone to sleep?"
"No, he's awake."
He stared back for a while in silence.
"Aziza!"
Again there was silence. The face alongside his smiled, then slowly slid back inside and disappeared. Her husband remained silent, his arms around the bars.

Suddenly he glanced behind him and quickly drew in his arms. He signaled to her to move away, then disappeared from the window.

She stepped back, though she remained standing looking up at the window.

After a while she seated herself on the stones and stretched out her leg. Taking out a breast, she suckled her child.

The shadow advanced halfway across the street. She saw that its fringe was touching her foot. She drew her foot back a little. The place was quiet and the washing that had been hung out gently swayed in the breeze.

When she looked at her foot again, she saw that the shadow clothed the tips of her toes. She stood up.

The soldier was still inside the tower; the toe of his boot could be seen at the edge of the wooden platform. Before reaching where the horse stood she glanced behind her, but the window was empty.

She looked quietly at the policeman: his eyes were closed, his hands on the pommel of the saddle. The horse stood motionless.

She walked down the narrow passageway toward the main street.

Confrontation

The black rock and the wide hole: two things he remembers well. The red disc of the sun touching the horizon; the tops of the pyramids and the date-palms flooded by the rays of the setting sun. His boss in the office once said to him, "One day you'll find someone has built a house on your land while you're asleep and you know nothing about it." So, esteemed boss, it seems that you and my wife suddenly know it all.

He gazed at the wire firmly fixed to wooden posts. Who would believe it?—a hut, a man, a child, a whole family. He left the rock and walked alongside the wire. He entered by a side gate made of thin wooden stakes and was met by a slight, cool breeze. Some chickens fled in alarm toward the hut, and a rabbit looked out from the door, then gave a jump and vanished. He contemplated the window of the small hut and its sloping roof, and a donkey and a goat standing on the other side of the hut, the goat's udder so full it almost touched the ground. As he pressed against his lower jaw, he thought: a solid hut that surely took some time to build. His swift glances came to rest on the man's back. Dignified and unhurried, he walked toward him.

Half of the sun's disc disappeared and the evening shadows advanced on the body of the giant pyramids. A halo of red light shone on the pale, yellow tops.

The man was bending over a large log of wood. Beside him were four small boxes. Suddenly he started. This was apparent from the way the saw came to a halt and from the stillness of his tensed shoulders, as though he had sensed the strange footsteps.

Confrontation

He turned around. The newcomer was taken by surprise by two bulging fish eyes and a face as wrinkled as cracked earth.

He continued walking toward him with short, unhurried steps.

The man wiped his hands on his worn trousers. He was wearing a vest with long sleeves and the hair of his chest was the color of dust.

The newcomer stared for an instant at the log of wood and at the man's flat feet placed wide apart in anticipation.

Suddenly he sensed that the man had guessed, in some manner or other, who he was, and he felt a malicious desire to delay the meeting of their eyes.

He raised his gaze without enthusiasm. He regarded the date-palms and the fields of clover. He let his glance wander over the fence that surrounded the piece of land, then looked at the hut. A woman was sitting behind it in front of a brazier, her head toward them. His nose picked up the smell of cooking. He frowned slightly. The door of the hut was open; it was dark inside. An amusing situation, it would be a subject for good conversation with his colleagues the next day, his boss exploding with laughter and shouting, "Didn't I tell you?" Without looking at the man he suddenly said, "Been here long?"

He watched the man gathering up his carpentry tools. The back of his neck as he bent over looked thick and dark brown.

"Spent much time here?"

The man raised his head. In a low, hoarse voice he said, "About a month, three, four."

"Four?"

He said it without anger. He put his head back and, with his hands clasped behind him, began walking slowly, as though he had lost interest in the man sitting there. His restless eyes fell on a tract of land that had been recently plowed. The black earth was arranged in parallel lines. He went round the plowed land. With the tip of his stick he fiddled with small

Confrontation

clods of mud. In a week's time building would begin, his wife had told him. "Ten flats will be enough for now. After some months we'll build ten more on top of them." There's a difference between living by paying rent and living in your own house. That gives one a feeling... a feeling of... of what? The world has become constricted. He should understand that. Thousands are being born every day. It was a big mistake to leave the piece of land idle; another year and this quiet place would be teeming with the bustle of people. He struck the ground sharply with his stick and headed toward the man.

"What are you going to plant it with?" he asked, indicating the plot with a gesture of the head.

The man brought his knees together. For a while he stared silently toward the plot of land. "Radishes, cabbages—anything."

The newcomer smiled. He contemplated the man's face scornfully. *The wretch has guessed the truth. Turn your face toward me. Perhaps now he's thinking it's merely a delusion—and yet it will come as a surprise.*

"You like the spot, so it seems."

A child rushed out from inside the hut. He came to a sudden stop and looked curiously at the visitor. Raising his gallabia above his chest with a hand, he passed his other one over his rounded stomach. Then he ran to the fence. The sitting man regarded him with annoyance. The young boy scratched his side and back. Suddenly he squatted down. The man picked up a stone. The boy tried to raise himself to his feet, then shook his head, smiling entreatingly. Once again he squatted down. The man threw the stone. The visitor, smiling, said amiably, "Your son?"

The man nodded his head.

The confounded man wants to make me believe he's keeping the place clean.

"And this wire, what's it for?"

The man raised his eyes inquiringly.

The visitor smiled. "The fact is I'm... this land is mine."

Confrontation

He smiled again. "We're going to begin to build in a week. But seeing as how you like the place, why don't we not build at all?"

The man remained calm before his ironically expectant gaze. Then, suddenly, he turned toward the log of wood and drew the carpentry tools between his feet.

Darkness began to advance from the eastern horizon.

The visitor muttered coldly, "A wire and a shack and some radishes—you should at least ask permission. You might at least say 'Hey, you fellows, you owners of the land . . . .'"

He felt the air brushing against the tooth with a hole in it. The man pulled at the saw and worked it into the end of the log. His son was sitting on the other end, swinging his legs in a quick, regular movement.

A round disc was cut off the log. The man turned it about in his hands and threw it to one side. The visitor muttered, as the saw once again plunged into the wood, "What's your home town?"

"Home town?"

The visitor touched his tooth with the tip of his tongue. Had his wife come with him and seen all this, who knows if the man would have remained sitting like this in front of her? Perhaps she would have sorted him out with the toe of her shoe.

In the morning she had told him she wanted to see the land for the last time before they began building.

Suddenly the silence was rent by the braying of a donkey. The visitor turned his head. The donkey was engaged in a scuffle with the goat. They were exchanging fierce kicks and had stirred around them a storm of dust. The boy rushed toward them. The visitor smiled, indicating his enjoyment of the scene.

"Look—in a week we'll be starting. That's to say you've only got a couple of days."

The boy returned and sat down opposite the visitor.

Confrontation

"Are you listening to me or not?"
"I'm listening, sir. I'm listening."
"Look around for another place for yourself."
"Where?"
"Look around. The thing is that after two or three days you're to collect up your belongings and go."
"Where to?"
"Where to? Just go. Put your shack on the back of your donkey and go. Surely it's nothing new for you?"

The fields of clover were swimming in a soft, gentle darkness; the shadows were lengthening and covered the tips of the pyramids. They had become just like other vast hills that lay within view. The visitor glanced anxiously at the gray sky and said, "A whole year—every single day of a whole twelve months."

Suddenly he shouted at the boy. "Lad, stop shaking your feet." The boy stopped for a moment, then went on.

"Do you know—if I were to ask you for a year's rent, how much do you think it would come to?" He was silent for a moment. "Well what does it matter? The fact is you should thank the Lord I didn't come along before now."

The man remained bent over the saw.

"A really fine state of affairs. Hey, man, are you listening to me?"

"I'm listening, sir."
"Then what's it all about?"
"Nothing at all, sir. Nothing."
"You mean to say that out of all the people's land you found only mine?"
"Doesn't everyone say this?"
"Everyone? All right, be fair: a while here, a while there."

The man rose to his feet. He looked for a moment in the direction of the hut. "Sir, I've been here a year."
"So what?"
"I've been a year here."
"And so what?"

Confrontation

"I kept on waiting—every day I'd tell myself, 'He'll come tomorrow, he'll come tomorrow'—and you don't come."

"I'm free to do as I like."

"Two months. Every day I waited for you. Every day. No one came. Every day. So after that I made the house and settled in. Then you come and tell me to get out?"

"That's just what I'm telling you—whether you like it or not."

The man looked at him in silence. The visitor felt a strange calm inside his mouth.

"Yes. If I come here or not—it's my land. I'm free to do as I like with it."

The man sat down on a box.

"So you've settled down?"

He gazed at him for a moment in silence.

"Tomorrow. I'm coming tomorrow, and by God if I just find you here!"

"Where shall I go?"

"So that's how it is! You know very well what you're up to."

"I've been here a year."

"A year? That's great—you think you've got some right?"

The man's lips quivered and he stared silently toward the plot of plowed land.

"I know your sort only too well—only too well."

"I've been here a year. How shall I take away all this?"

"And why take it away? I'm wrong—tomorrow I won't be coming. There's a government. I won't be coming. The year's rent—tomorrow. I'll sell off these things, one by one. I'm wrong—what I'll do is . . . ."

He fell silent. He felt he was on the point of committing some folly. Suddenly, controlling his heavy breathing, he spun round.

The man followed him with his eyes as he crossed the ground with wide, stumbling strides. He gathered up his carpentry tools and, shouldering them, went toward the hut.

Confrontation

The boy looked in the direction taken by the visitor. The road was empty. He let down his gallabia over his thighs and threw a stone over the fence, then ran and caught up his father.

Uncle Zeydan

Uncle Zeydan returned.
He stood in front of the dilapidated house and took down the saddlebag from the donkey's back. It was a house without an owner: it looked like a ruin, without roof or doors.

My mother said: "He . . . he's your uncle. He now has a long beard and a cloak."

"Why doesn't he come and stay with us?" I asked.

She would sit in front of the hearth, blowing into the fire, her eyes watering with the smoke.

She said he had gone off when I was still crawling. He had taken the money from my grandfather and had journeyed off to bring back barley, but hadn't returned.

In the house, too, they hadn't talked about him all these years. My grandfather, when something came up that reminded him, would suddenly scowl and have a fit of coughing.

❖

He stood in front of the dilapidated house. Uncle Zeydan was shifting to one side the stones that had fallen down in one of the rooms. He turned and saw me and motioned to me to enter. I ran back home. I saw him again as he was going out: he wanted to cross the dry water-channel in front of the house; he bent down and moved the donkey's front feet onto the other bank, at which it made the jump. I was on the roof of our house and I went down hurriedly and ran after him. The donkey was veering toward the side of the road and scraping against the trees.

Uncle Zeydan

"Is it blind?" I asked.

He nodded in silence. He was staring into my face and he asked me: "Do you know who I am?"

"You're Uncle Zeydan."

"And who told you? Your grandfather?"

"My grandfather doesn't say. My father saw you as you were coming. Why did you buy it?"

"Is it he who's calling you?"

I turned round and saw my father in front of our house waving at me. I went back at a run.

My father hurled me down violently and I fell among the legs of the cattle. As I crawled away I saw him bending down to the ground, and I heard my grandfather shout: "Hit him, the son of a dog."

Then I saw my father advancing, the branch of a tree in his hand. I jumped onto the wall of the courtyard and climbed up onto the cattle shack. My mother shouted and ran toward us pulling my father away.

"Don't let me see you talking to that man again," he roared.

My mother dried the wound on my head with earth from the oven and led me off by the hand to the bedroom.

My grandfather and I slept in the one room. He had attacks of coughing during the night and my mother placed a pitcher of water alongside me. When the coughing fit got worse and he was incapable of calling me, I would suddenly wake up. After a gulp of water he would calm down and I would go back to sleep.

Early in the morning my father would carry him in his woolen cloak and take him out into the courtyard, where my mother would have prepared him a bed of straw. When the weather was warm, he would take him out to the stone bench. He would seem so small on my father's shoulder, his flabby legs uncovered and looking exceedingly thin. My mother, too, was easily able to carry him. She would raise him up by his armpits and drag him away from the straw

Uncle Zeydan

which he had wetted when he was seated in the courtyard. She would take off the wet wrap around his loins and put on a dry one. My grandfather would thrust his face to the wall. Sensing my presence, he would whisper to my mother, without turning: "The boy."

My mother would turn round and scold me, telling me to go away.

My grandfather had stopped going out to the stone bench ever since Uncle Zeydan came. He would sit in the corner of the courtyard, the brazier beside him, and holding a long stick with which he would strike out at the chickens and ducks that approached him and at the dogs that sometimes crept in from outside when he was having a nap to sniff at him and lick his face.

He would awaken at my mother's footsteps and ask her who had passed by the house and whose voices he had heard a short while ago. And when he saw me in front of him, he would ask whether it was so-and-so who had passed by just now and I would say that it was.

He would close his eyes and, adjusting the cloak round his body, go back to his slumbers.

❖

My father would carry him at night after supper to the stone bench. At that moment my grandfather would look overjoyed. My mother would seat herself at the threshold and I would stretch out alongside her. My grandfather would point at the extensive fields and say: "All of them were wasteland."

And my father would say: "Yes, wasteland."

And my grandfather would say: "If I'd only known at the time I would have bought a hundred feddans. I had the money. Abbas bought twenty feddans, and Gaber too. Yes, the feddan was going for milliemes. Fifty piasters—and not a drop of water. Who was to know that afterward they would dig the irrigation canal? I told them: 'And from where are you going to get the money for it? Five's enough.'"

Uncle Zeydan

And my father says: "It all turned out for the best."
And my grandfather says: "Thanks be to God."
And the two of them fall silent. Then I hear the gentle snoring of my grandfather, and my father carries him inside.

❖

It was the first time they talked about Uncle Zeydan. It had been a week since he had come and we were having supper in the courtyard.
"He's still here?" said my grandfather.
"Oh yes," said my father.
"And what brought him?"
"God knows."
"Didn't you meet up with him?"
"I did. Two days ago. He was standing at Abd al-Samad's, the grocer."
Their voices were low, their eyes on their food. My grandfather said, "And what did you talk about?"
"We didn't talk. I bought tobacco and went off."
"Why Abd al-Samad's shop?"
"I only saw him when I was inside the shop."
"And he didn't say anything?"
"Nothing. He went on looking at me till I left."

❖

My grandfather couldn't bear to be away from the stone bench for long. My father put down a mattress for him by the courtyard's outer door. He left the door slightly open. As he looked out at the fields, his eyes looked as if he was on the point of falling asleep. When he discovered that something extraneous had crept into the wide scene that extended before him, he would question my father and mother and would beard passers-by. For days before the return of Uncle Zeydan, he had kept pointing at the broad canal alongside the maize, saying, "They haven't released the water yet. What is al-Dugheidi up to?"
My father and mother didn't pay attention to what he was saying. He would stare into their faces questioningly. Al-

Uncle Zeydan

Dugheidi's land was a distance of three plots away. It drew its water from the canal.

One day my father told him that he had asked al-Dugheidi and that the man was searching around for laborers.

❖

My grandfather was angry. "Do the laborers have to be from the village? He'd do better to spend some money and bring them in from another village."

My mother brought him his tea beside the door. He was overjoyed to discover that during his absence from the stone bench they had cut down the mulberry tree. It was an enormous tree with thick branches and stood between two fields facing us. My grandfather used to say that there was something strange about it being there and that its roots stretched into the field and weakened the crop. His head, protruding from the opening of the cloak, looked small and smooth. He was pointing with his hand and saying to my mother, "At last they've cut it down. Look. They used to say there was no other shade in the fields."

On this day he seemed to have forgotten that Uncle Zeydan had returned. He was laughing and teasing me with the stick. At supper he told us about the vast trees he had seen in the Sudan and how the people would go to sleep among their branches.

❖

My grandfather discovered my place on top of the roof. I would stretch out there in the morning among the heaps of straw, staring down at the dilapidated house where Uncle Zeydan was living. I would see him there, amid the stones that had fallen down, getting his things together in the corner of the room before going out. My grandfather watched me for a long time when I got down off the roof. I felt his eyes following me as I crossed the courtyard. He raged at me as I approached and he took up the stick from beside him.

He said to my father: "Take the boy with you. Don't leave him here."

❖

Uncle Zeydan

The blaze of the fire lit up the entrance to the dilapidated house. I stood for a moment in hesitation, then went in. Uncle Zeydan was lying down, his face close to the fire. He indicated a flat stone alongside him. I sat down and he said, "Are you Ibrahim?"

He was very much like my grandfather: the same pointed nose, small watering eyes and thick eyebrows. He said in a quiet voice, "Do they beat you when you come here?"

He put some small pieces of wood on the fire. Some of the smoke was trailing up into his face.

"You've got your father's long hands and his wide mouth. Does he still go to sleep with rice in his mouth?"

He fell silent. He was staring into my face as he said, "Have you seen your grandfather's trunk?"

Again he fell silent, then said, "The large black trunk in the corner of the reception room with the black padlock. For three years he carried it about on his back far and wide. Didn't he tell you? Have you seen what's in the trunk? Yellow buttons the color of gold. Did he tell you they were gold? And empty cartridge cases and pieces of shrapnel. And the bronze medal in its black case. He hasn't told you how they awarded him the medal?"

He was moving the fire with the tip of his finger. I said I had seen the trunk.

"And the medal?"
"And the medal."
"And the buttons?"
"And the buttons."
"And the empty cartridge cases?"
"And the empty cartridge cases."
He smiled. "And the black soldier up in the tree . . ."
He laughed and I rushed out.

❖

My grandfather said that he was over there.

He took hold of my father's arm, pointing to the sycamore tree by the river.

Uncle Zeydan

My father said that he too had seen him.

He looked through the open doorway, then turned to my grandfather. My grandfather looked at him with flickering eyes and whispered, "Yesterday he was there too. He returned from among the fields opposite to us and his eyes were on the house all the time. He passed by the door, which was open, and stared into my face."

My father said, "Do you want me to move you away from the door?"

"Yes."

My father moved the bedding to the corner of the courtyard, carrying my grandfather on his shoulder.

"He'll kill me," said my grandfather. "He's come to kill me."

My father placed him on the bedding, wrapping him round with the cloak.

"Leave the boy," said my grandfather. "Don't take him with you."

❖

My father said that three years ago Uncle Zeydan had sent some men to my grandfather. They met up with him in the mosque. My grandfather refused to talk to them; he left them and made off.

My mother said, "You didn't tell me before."

My father said that he too had known only today, when my grandfather had told him.

My mother said, "And what did they want?"

My father said that my grandfather didn't tell him.

The two of them were talking in a whisper on the stone bench. My grandfather was asleep in the room.

❖

At night the blaze of the fire gushes out in front of the dilapidated house, the light extending halfway into the field in front. Uncle Zeydan has returned to the house. Suddenly my grandfather fell silent, looking over my father's shoulder

Uncle Zeydan

at the light. The intensity of the dark over the fields is less—I was even aware of the dark shadows of those trees by the river. My mother whispers in a low voice, "He keeps it alight all night long."

Only I heard her: I was lying down, my head on her lap.

❖

Early in the morning I would see Uncle Zeydan from the top of the roof going off with his donkey to the sycamore tree, taking off his clothes as he retired behind it, bending down low and dragging the donkey to the water, the glistening spray flying up. He used to cross the river and strike at the water with his feet as he swam with the current. On his return he would cut through the fields, his head bare and the shawl hanging down over his shoulder, with the donkey stumbling behind him on the raised edge of the field. He would give me a fleeting glance in my place on the roof. As he advanced, he would look as though he were taking the house by storm. I would see my grandfather in the corner of the courtyard having suddenly woken from his sleep, as though he had heard the puffing of the donkey, and staring in the direction of the courtyard door expectantly. Uncle Zeydan would pass by the house and move on.

❖

My grandfather said that he hears him at night as he passes behind the house to the fields. He asked my father what he was doing there.

My father was warming his hands over the blaze of the fire. He kept silent.

My grandfather said that he also hears him when he is coming back, and he looked at my father's face inquiringly.

The weather was cold. My mother placed the roll of hot bran around his middle, and my father carried him to the bedroom.

In the morning my grandfather stayed on in the room and my mother carried the brazier in to him.

Uncle Zeydan

❖

I woke up in the night to the sound of his racking cough. I saw him seated in the bed, his cloak having fallen from his body. His shoulder looked bare through the opening in the gallabia.

I asked him if he wanted a drink.

He motioned me to keep silent. He was breathing heavily and had raised his head expectantly. I heard a noise outside like that of the wind touching the tops of the crops. Then it seemed to me that it was the sound of breathing up against the window. I was staring at my grandfather, then I fell asleep.

When my father entered the room in the morning he found him dead.

❖

Uncle Zeydan collected his belongings and put them into the two openings of the saddlebag. I was stretched out on the roof and the courtyard was crowded with women and men making ready for the funeral.

Uncle Zeydan lifted up the saddlebag. He stood for a while, silent and with bowed head. Then, turning, he pulled at the donkey and went off.

That's How it Was

Hagg Enani said he was responsible for his men's debts. The letter was a short one and had been sent to Mr. Madbuli, the headmaster of the elementary school. He had received it when he was in the courtyard of the mosque after Friday prayers, just as he was about to go out. He stood there at a loss as to why Hagg Enani should have chosen him of all people to communicate the message to, when he had never met him and was not owed any money by his men.

He saw them in the mosque gathered round the letter. He remained standing by the door, his eyes fixed on the letter until it was returned to him. He folded it up into the silk-lined pocket of his wallet, and left without saying a word.

The village people took it as a good omen, for Hagg Enani's men were not like God's simple creatures; he would track them down one by one from places the villagers had neither seen nor heard of. Whenever a gang of itinerant workers came to dredge the river, they would leave the village with three or four of their number missing. The overseer of Hagg Enani's farm would often declare—after a heavy evening session in the café, twirling his mustache and with his reddened eyes looking right and left and behind him at a cluster of the farm men—that the men of the village were good for nothing except cleaning out the plots of land and collecting up the dung. He would spit as he uttered an oath, and they would all ride off in a gharry to the farm. He used to come with the skilled workers who operated the tractors and machines at the farm to spend the evening in the village.

That's How it Was

They would move from café to café, and he would take a folded handkerchief from his pocket and put it on the table top, opening it slowly, with all eyes gazing at him, to reveal a piece of hashish the size of half a hand. He would cut at it with a small penknife in the shape of a fish and collect up the crumbs and chew them. They would walk noisily through the streets, hurling obscenities at the closed windows, and then make off for the river. They would end up soaked at the railing of the bridge, where they would make comments about the passers-by, at which the local men would leave the railing one after the other.

They would take what they needed from the shops on credit. At the beginning they used to pay, but then their debts filled the shopkeepers' ledgers, who would nevertheless continue to give them what they wanted.

The overseer would look after the affairs of the farm, while Hagg Enani would come to spend a month there in the summer and then depart. The people would see his blue car darting through the village streets, the curtains drawn across the windows. They would see him again at the end of the month rushing past on his way back to the city.

Uncle Shakir the grocer heard what had happened and nipped off to see Abd al-Samie the cloth merchant.

"Have you heard?"

"Yes, I have."

They stood together on the raised mud platform outside the shop. Uncle Shakir pushed his skull-cap to the back of his head and said, "Has anyone been there?"

"God alone knows."

Uncle Shakir, with his bulging eyes, was searching his face.

"And what about going ourselves?" he said.

Each gazed at the other.

The weather was hot, the sun flooding the platform and the entrance to the shop.

"Let's wait a little," said Abd al-Samie.

That's How it Was

"What are we waiting for? Didn't he send a message to Mr. Madbuli?"

In the end they agreed to go to the farm early the following morning.

Each of them put on shoes and a clean gallabia and carried his ledger wrapped in a towel under his arm. Round his neck Uncle Shakir wore a scarf made of shimmering cloth. The two of them went out to the main road and walked along a strip of dried weeds, avoiding the dust. Suddenly Abd al-Samie came to a stop and, stretching out his thin neck, said with a scowl, "You didn't say you'd be wearing a scarf."

Uncle Shakir also came to a stop, and his gaze fled off toward the tree-tops.

"I've not seen you wearing it before," growled Abd al-Samie. "Where did you get it from?"

"I had it."

They crossed a bridge leading to a narrow path through the fields; they walked side by side.

"How much are you owed?" said Abd al-Samie.

"Twenty pounds and forty-three piasters."

"And what did they buy with all that money?"

"Cigarettes. Cheese. Sweets. And what are you owed?"

"A lot."

"How much?"

"Forty-five."

There were silent for a while.

"Do you think he'll pay off the whole sum?" said Abd al-Samie.

"Why not?"

"Perhaps he'll think my amount is too big."

They drank from a large earthenware water jug that was standing under a tree, and Uncle Shakir wiped the sweat and dust from his face with a clean handkerchief he took from his pocket. Abd al-Samie was looking at him in silence, then he said, "Let's have a look at your ledger."

Uncle Shakir gave him a reluctant look, and Abd al-Samie said, "Here's my ledger—take it."

That's How it Was

Each took the other's ledger as they stood in the shade of the tree. Abd al-Samie's handwriting was slanted, with the words ending in flourishes and with the final vowel sounds marked in. At the end of each page he had entered, inside a small square marked in red, the total amount, which he had also written out in words. In Uncle Shakir's ledger the writing was indistinct. The ink he had used was faded and the ends of the letters were broken off abruptly, while the figures were squeezed in between the words.

"Let's hurry up before the sun gets too high," said Abd al-Samie.

Uncle Shakir caught up with him. "Do you think he'll be able to read the ledger?"

"What's it matter? You read it out to him."

"How? Do you think he'll wait for me to read it?"

"Put a mark in the ledger as of now."

They each placed a small piece of straw at the page where the debt was shown.

The large house appeared before them. It was surrounded by tall eucalyptus trees and had a white facade, pillars, and a wide veranda. There were small towers of colored glass on top of the roof, in the center of which was a large dome that threw off a colored reflection.

They stood at the bend in the road, staring ahead in silence, the barking of dogs reverberating among the trees.

The Trap

We were contained within the dark space under the bed he had indicated to us. The bed was high, with black supports, each of which was decorated with an engraved branch of a tree in white, coiling up like a snake, with its knots and little leaves; the mosquito net was folded up to one side. We squatted there with our heads almost touching the wooden base. "He'll come in a little while and you'll see him," he had said to us.

There were days when he would try to come with us. In order to spur us on, he had said that the patrol officer carried the biggest revolver you could possibly see and four daggers hanging to his side. We didn't believe him, for we would often see the patrol as it passed at night. We had finished our afternoon stroll. We had passed by the mulberry trees and he hadn't had the courage to climb them with us. He had stood underneath them, making do with those fruit that fell after we had shaken the outlying branches, collecting them and blowing the dust from them. And when we made our way to the canal, he had sat on the bank guarding our clothes. This time we had promised to go with him and so he kept following us, and we chased after a mangy dog until it fled into the fields, and when it was dark we went with him.

From a bundle he brought from inside the house he produced some cheese and fresh rounds of bread, which he put before us. We ate without speaking. He did not eat. He was alert to the sounds outside, leaning with his arm on a large box closed with a rusty lock. He said that inside it were

The Trap

the clothes of his deceased father, who had been an employee at the municipal council and who used to stop him playing with us. The boy would stand far off at the top of the street watching us in his clean gallabia and shoes, his hair neatly combed. Sometimes he would look down from the roof of their house and call to us to play in front of him, letting down a long rope which he could move about from side to side. That, though, did not induce us to go to him. After the death of his father he told us that he was now able to play with us. After some days, however, his mother stopped him. "It's the wish of the deceased," she had said.

After eating we felt tired, so we went to sleep. He woke us by gently shaking us. We could hear the whinnying of the horses outside, then we saw a light entering the room. It was his mother carrying the lamp. We knew it was her from the black slippers and the end of her black gallabia: we sometimes used to see her when she was on her way to the station, carrying a yellow envelope in her hand, to take the train to the city. She hung the lamp somewhere on the wall and dragged in behind her two cane chairs, then went out.

We would always find that there were three of them as they passed by. The officer had one pip on his shoulder and wore his cap tilted slightly back, showing his thinning ash-colored hair, and had a thick gray moustache, in the middle of which was a dark mark from smoking. Behind him were two straight-backed soldiers. Their voices came to us from close by the window, though we couldn't distinguish them.

One of them entered the room, and the boy alongside us started and motioned to us. We had, however, seen the black shoes treading on the rug. The floor of the room was of mud and uneven; the rug had grown thin where there were bulges, the small ones sticking out like rats' heads. The shoes vanished from sight, then returned, though without coming to a stop. We leaned forward and bent down to follow him with our eyes, for he was screened by the hanging sheet when he went in the direction of the window at the far end of the

The Trap

room. At last he stood with his back to us, the rug rucked up under his heels—no doubt there was a small hole there. He began rocking backward and forward, with the leather-covered stick striking at the side of his khaki trousers. We heard her voice saying: "I was giving the two soldiers some tea."

There was a couch by the opposite wall, which we had noticed on entering. Behind it was the sill of the wide window, on which were placed two pitchers of water, each in a tin saucer. As we leaned forward we were almost flat on the ground. The two of them were sitting on the couch with two small cushions between them. She was on the end, her legs drawn together and her hands clasped in her lap, while he was resting against the back of the couch with his legs outstretched.

"They told me you were at our place today."

"Yes. I thought that maybe they'd changed their minds."

"Changed their minds? I've told you a thousand times that there are such things as laws."

"Yes, you told me."

"He only had a few years of service."

"Yes."

"They don't qualify him for a pension. I've told you."

"Yes."

"You don't listen to what I say."

From the movement of his legs it seemed that he was leaning toward her and had placed the two cushions under his arm and had his hand held over hers.

"Someone like you who's been brought up in the city, what brought you here?"

He drew her hand toward him, then freed it from his grasp and put it back in her lap. He took hold of her wrist and, standing up, pulled her to her feet.

"An exceptional pension, as I told you. There's no other solution. And the investigations, I write them myself."

He pushed her toward the bed. When she turned round,

The Trap

traces of flour could be seen in the light on her gallabia. He leaned over to dust them off.

"Still wearing this gallabia?"

He removed the wisps of straw clinging to her back, then made as if to take it off her. She removed his hand. He wanted to undo the black head-dress and she leaned away from his hand. Her toes were contracted as they clung to the slippers. We had stretched out our heads a little, hidden behind the sheet that was hanging down. He was lifting her up from under her arms, pushing her to the bed. When she leaned over to climb up, his face suddenly appeared urgently from behind her. We drew our heads back inside and caught a glimpse of him, before we disappeared, as he took the slippers from her feet. He pushed his boots to one side and his trousers fell in a heap at his feet. His legs were exceedingly thin, their skin soft and the color of wax and with black socks mended at the big toe. We held our breath and hunched up our legs, crouching back so that we were almost touching the wall. The boy was still leaning his arms on the box, his eyes ablaze. He no longer paid us any attention but had his head bent slightly as he listened intently to the slight quivering of the bed and the creaking of the wooden mattress base, and to the man's breathless whispering: "That always happens— but just let me get used to you."

The sound of the coughing of the two soldiers outside and the horses shaking their heads and breathing heavily and rubbing their necks against the base of the window.

His thin legs slid down and disappeared inside the trousers.

We waited for a while after he left until we heard the sound of the horses moving off.

The door was ajar. We looked at the boy. He met our gaze with eyes heavy with sleep. One after the other, we crept outside.

Meeting

The old woman told him a man was waiting for him.

It was night and a faint light showed in the courtyard of the house where the old woman was sleeping. He went up the stairs and felt the cold air stinging his face as he crossed the roof to his room.

He saw him over there in the corner in front of his room seated on a low chair, brought no doubt by the old woman. He was wrapped in an overcoat, his head to the wall.

He opened the door of the room and put on the light, then went out and woke the man. The man, running his hand over a cloth suitcase beside him, called out cheerfully, "At last—Mr. Khalil."

He rose slowly and followed him inside. The room was narrow and had no windows; there was a small bed, a chair, and a table on which were some dusty books.

Khalil drew out the chair and seated himself on the edge of the bed. The man remained standing, looking around him. In the light the overcoat seemed colorless; it was growing thin at the elbows. He dried his watering eyes and once again shrank back into the overcoat.

"I've waited for hours for you. The old lady told me you were coming at nine, so I waited. Don't you remember me?"

"Mr. Bashir."

The man's face glowed with pleasure. "I asked in the village about your address—Hagg Ahmad at the post office gave it to me and said you were working in the Blue Bird store. I told myself I'd wait for you here. It's years since you paid a visit to the village."

Meeting

He sat on the chair and looked at the books. Then, from his overcoat pocket, he took out a pair of glasses with some tape stuck round one arm.

"Ah, many years. I remember you when you were in short trousers. All of you I always remember in short trousers. And some of you have married and have children in school. Oh, what days they were! You were among the best students in my form and I always said you had a great future awaiting you. I remember the day I had you read out your composition in class."

He dabbed at his mouth and nose, while Khalil clasped his hands between his legs. The cold air was gusting along the ground and under the bed.

"That day the headmaster was in the class and applauded you. He was the first to clap—God rest his soul. He was a good man. That day he asked me, 'Is he in your form?' And he said, 'It's a good idea to have outstanding essays read out in class.' I was the originator of the idea—and he adjusted the dental plate in his mouth with the tip of his little finger.

"And you live here?"

He looked around for a moment.

"And that day when I called you from the third form. The boys in the fourth didn't know how to solve a problem in arithmetic. I remember it was a problem of multiplying simple fractions. I said, 'I'll call someone from the third form who'll solve it for you' —and I called you. Just imagine if you hadn't been able to solve it! I sent the messenger boy for you. When you entered the class I said to the boys, 'Give him a clap' —and you were taken aback. I saw you standing by the door in confusion and I said, 'Come along, Khalil,' and I stood you alongside me for a while, then I gave you a piece of colored chalk. I turned my back on you—oh, what would have happened if you'd made a mistake in trying to solve it! I was leaning my hand on the desk, looking at the boys. I saw in their eyes that you had finished. I asked without turning around, 'What's the answer?' And you said . . . you said . . . .'

Meeting

And Khalil said in a whisper, "Eight and a half."

"Eight and a half." And I said without turning round, 'Correct.' And I said to the boys, 'Give him a clap.' I wanted to give you something, but what? I was at a loss. Then I saw the colored chalk—red and blue. I preceded you to the door. 'We thank you, Khalil. Go back to your form.'"

He leaned back: he was jogging his crossed legs.

"Fancy if you'd made a mistake!"

He laughed and looked at Khalil, who was still in his work clothes: the grey jacket with a circle on the chest of white cloth in the middle of which was a small bird in blue with outstretched wings.

"So you live here?"

He looked around him. The walls were of a dull rose color; the lower part bulged where the paint had peeled off. In the middle of the wall opposite the door was fixed a sheet of thick blue paper that appeared to be hiding a gap in the wall; behind the door, pajamas, a towel, and a pair of trousers were hanging.

"This is the second time I've been to Cairo. The first time was ten years ago and I returned on the same day."

He laughed. "This time I'll only return after several years. I've got a contract to work abroad." —and he brought together the two ends of his overcoat above his knees.

"I have three years to go before retiring. I said to myself 'Go.' I'm traveling tomorrow. The plane leaves at . . . ."

He stretched out his hand and took some papers from his pocket.

"I can't read the figures they write on their tickets. Look. Nine in the morning, isn't that so?"

Khalil raised his head. He looked as though he were listening to some noise outside. The wind was playing with some empty tins on the roof. His face was thin and intensely pallid, with tiny wrinkles round the mouth. Khalil said in a low voice, "The place here isn't big enough."

Mr. Bashir returned the papers to his pocket and laughed. "I'll not put you to any inconvenience. I'll stay here in the chair."

Meeting

They exchanged glances in silence. Mr. Bashir said, "If it won't inconvenience you."

Khalil looked as though he were still listening to the sound of the wind outside. His eyelids were drooping. Mr. Bashir stretched out his hand and ran it over the suitcase. Placing it on his knees, he opened the zip, then closed it.

"Maybe I did something wrong?" he muttered.

Khalil remained silent.

Mr. Bashir rose to his feet and made for the door. He turned round and they again exchanged glances in silence. Khalil was still sitting on the edge of the bed, his hands clasped between his legs. Then Mr. Bashir went out and closed the door.

Hagg Abd Rabbuh

Hagg Abd Rabbuh thought, on his return from the settlement, to make a short cut. The sun was scorching and there was no breeze. He crossed through the patches of land, pushing away with his thin stick the leaves of the sugar cane that were hanging over the dikes. He came up to a narrow dirt track and a water-course that widened as it approached the village. He heard the faint sound of singing coming from the small bridge. The sycamore tree gave shade to the place there, and he saw the gallabia spread out on its sloping branch. On drawing nearer, he caught sight of the girl in the water-course, leaning over a white rock and scrubbing her clothes. She was naked, the water up to her middle. Her body was small and thin and of a pale whiteness with a slight yellow tinge to it, and her breasts were like two lemons. He was encompassed by a silence that was more like a state of trance. Everything looked brilliantly familiar, bringing back a dream he had had many times.

"What is it, Hagg? What is it?"

She was covering her breasts with her arms, while a smile wavered on her face. He bent over, stretching out his hands. He made a trembling, gulping sound and lifted her from the water. The body was submissive in his hands. He laid her down on the viscid mud.

The village houses came into view at last. He contemplated them as he stood in the shade of a tree. The familiar scene:

Hagg Abd Rabbuh

irregular roofs and a minaret. He rubbed the mud from his gallabia. He was leaning over removing the mud that had stuck to his under-trousers when he saw her: it was as if she had burst out from the darkness of undefined shadows. The brightness was suddenly extinguished. He stared with glazed eyes. She was hurrying along the track, her wet gallabia clinging to her body and hampering her progress. She was squeezing out her underpants as she walked. She slowed her pace as she approached him. She placed her feet through the openings in her underpants and drew them up. With a morose face he stormed at her, "Get away, girl. Get away."

"Where shall I get away to, Hagg?"

He turned round to the road, heaving with violent rage. He looked behind him and saw her there. Suddenly he went back to her and rained blows on her with his thin stick. The girl, bending over, took the blows on her arm without a sound. He was breathing heavily, his eyes blank. His corpulent body did not help him. He felt heavy as he walked to where he could make out the canal waters. Sitting on the bank with his back to the road, he collected his breath. The girl was standing a few steps away rubbing her arm. He moistened his face and got to his feet. He walked in the direction of the village. He did not turn round but was conscious of her behind him.

❖

The open space in front of the house teemed with men gathered round the platform scales. Bales of cotton were leaning against the balcony wall, with young boys sitting on them. His three sons were standing between the supports of the scales and the husbands of his four daughters were alongside them beyond the supports. One of them was holding the account book and pen. A bale was hanging on the scales, gently swaying. He slowed down a little as he noticed that the end of the bale was scraping against the ground. Everyone fell silent as he passed by them and they answered his silent salutation. He continued looking at the suspended

Hagg Abd Rabbuh

bale and saw them raising it from the ground. His middle son approached him with long strides, as though to tell him something, but when he saw him continuing on his way he stopped. He always preferred to use the back door when the men were collected in front of the balcony, as they would stop him and indulge in a lot of talk, sometimes slipping off inside behind him. Without really meaning to, he had gradually distanced himself from them. And they, feeling this, no longer asked too much of him. Sometimes after the evening prayer they would inform him, in a few words, of what they had accomplished. He would listen for a moment, surprised at his unconcern, blaming himself and determined to return to his place among them on the balcony. He would meet up with them as he made his tour of the fields, greeting them from afar, and when they saw that he had paused they would approach him, saying something and laughing a little, and follow him as he continued on his way until he went out to the road. He would wander about by force of habit, making for places that were familiar to him and old friends who suddenly came to mind. In going to see them he would relive far-off days and moments that suddenly took on a sparkle; when excited he would laugh and turn to the shaded side of the road, moving leisurely and collecting up the brittle yellow leaves of the trees and crumbling them up in his hands and scattering them. As soon as the faraway voices had vanished he would stand quietly staring about him, then he would turn around and go back.

The back door of the house is always open: children and women go in and out. As he draws near he feels tired—fatigue has come on him suddenly. There are many women in the courtyard: his daughters and his son's women, also the women of the men working on his land, and of neighbors. Many of the women he doesn't know, even with many of his sons' women he gets muddled up and can't distinguish his youngest son's wife from his eldest's. Ever since his wife fell

Hagg Abd Rabbuh

on the stairs she had been gathering them around her. She had chosen for herself the room near the front door, where she lay in bed with half her body paralyzed. He had entered it only once, years ago, two months after the accident. He had wanted to see her and had chosen the time of dawn when everyone would be sleeping. The door of the room was half open. He pushed it a little and it creaked loudly. A lamp was hanging on the wall, glowing faintly. Women were lying together on the mat, their heads in the direction of the bed. One of them at the end had the coverlet lifted and her buttocks were exposed. He stood in hesitation by the door. His eyes met those of his wife. As always, she woke at the same time as he. Once again they exchanged looks. Drawing the door to, he returned to his room.

Despite the many different hands working in the house he found everything as he was accustomed to and would sense her presence behind it all.

His room was deep inside the house, far from bustle and noise. The women in the courtyard stood to one side when he passed by. There were many rooms here and there where his sons lived. No sooner had he changed his gallabia than he heard a rapping on the door. It would be one of his daughters or his son's women—for some time he had ceased to ask who it was—bearing the tray of food. She would seat herself at the threshold until he had finished, the basin and ewer beside her.

❖

After his afternoon nap he made his way outside. The courtyard was empty and the sun on the horizon had begun to take on color. Girls sat in front of the balcony playing with pebbles. He passed by them, then became aware of two eyes staring at him. He turned. He recognized her from the long scar under her left ear. She was sitting cross-legged, playing jack-stones and repeating words he did not understand. She was swaying her small body to right and left, rising up on her knees, while the girls around her cheered excitedly. He stood

Hagg Abd Rabbuh

for a moment in hesitation. The girl was immersed in her play and paid him no attention. He continued on his way.

He settled down in front of the wood storehouse on the bank of the river. With him was Hagg Salih, the owner of the storehouse; they sat on two couches facing one another, chatting and drinking tea.

"Yes—days that won't come back."

"That's true."

And they fell silent.

Hagg Salih was leaning his weight on his stick. He smiled, his watchful eyes on the door of the storehouse, which was fully open.

"Mad," he says.

"Who's to tell."

"He sold the whole lot. He didn't keep a single qirat."

"Who's to tell, Hagg Salih."

"He's now got four trucks. That's one of them," and he pointed at a truck standing in front of the storehouse. It was open from the back and some workmen were coming in and out loading planks of wood.

"His name's on the door, and the name of his son, and his address, and an office with a telephone, and he says, 'To hell with land and those who want it.'"

Hagg Abd Rabbuh leaned back a bit, stretching out his legs on the couch and resting his back against the arm. He contemplated the truck. One of the men was leaning over the front, wiping it with a rag.

"Is that him?"

"Yes, it is."

"And how much does he take per load?"

"It varies, but he's making good money."

He was on the point of looking again when he saw her. She was over there, a few paces from the workmen, following their movements. He no longer mistook her after seeing her in front of the house—the faded gallabia with the rose that had retained its blueness on the chest, torn at the shoulder;

Hagg Abd Rabbuh

the black, unruly hair; the dust-covered legs; and the white splotches on her pallid cheeks.

Two workmen came out of the storehouse carrying planks between them on their shoulders. She darted between them, bent over, and looked at him laughingly. She brushed her hand over the back of her gallabia and advanced to where the two of them were sitting. She passed by them to the bank. She held on to the trunk of a tree and turned around. He was looking back, watching her. They exchanged looks. She was standing leaning her shoulder against the trunk of the tree, her feet crossed. He sat up straight, scowling, as he searched round with his foot for his shoe under the couch. When he looked again she had disappeared.

His peace disturbed, he no longer wanted to stay on. He walked along the bank, making for the café. The dying light of sunset and the dark waters of the river. As he dried the sticky sweat on his face with the end of his wide sleeve, he saw her. She was over there, crouching under a tree near the prayer-room, throwing pebbles at the river. Her singing suddenly stopped, so it seemed she was aware of his approach. She turned and began watching him silently. He tried to appear calm, then all of a sudden gave a scowl and leaned over and picked up a stone, "Get away, girl. Get away."

"Where shall I get away to, Hagg?"

She crawled out of range of the stone, then jumped to her feet and, darting in front of him, disappeared into a side alley. He stood breathing heavily and staring into the alley.

❖

The uproar inside the café was intense. They were playing cards and shouting. Not once had he come to it and found it quiet. He dragged a chair to the river bank. They were hanging a hurricane lamp on the bough of a tree; in its light rats could be seen running among the bare branches. Some men were sitting at a table playing chess—teachers and clerks at the local council, men who didn't play cards or backgammon like the

Hagg Abd Rabbuh

others. He seated himself not far off and smoked a water-pipe, his foot on another chair, listening to their chatter. It was the same talk they never tired of. He nevertheless liked listening to them. He found himself laughing when they did. One of them shouted, "Isn't that so, Hagg?"

The salary that isn't sufficient, and the yearly raise that is useless because of the steep rise in prices, the tour of work abroad that doesn't come, but might transport them to the other side of the river. And they look at the other bank, where the new suburb lies: small one- and two-storied houses with Indian fig trees cut to weird shapes in front of them within squares surrounded by low walls, and the flat roofs slightly sloping so that the rain can run off them, and the television aerials erected on them like scarecrows.

"Simplicity is the characteristic of the age."

"And the Indian fig."

"And reinforced concrete."

"And why reinforced?"

"Better than your folks' houses, which are like rats' holes where you can lose yourself."

One of them, who had remained silent all the while, suddenly said, with his hands in his coat pocket, "And what's it got to do with Abd al-Nasser?"

They turned to him, taken by surprise.

"God have mercy upon his soul. Did someone mention him?"

A cool breeze was rising from the river and the live coal of the water-pipe had gone out. He was overcome by sleep and was woken by the sound that emanated from him. He rose to his feet. In a trance of drowsiness he walked off, feeling his way along the bank, avoiding entering the café. He spotted her before she was aware of him; she was crouching behind the café humming in a low voice. She quickly got to her feet and flexed herself to jump. He raged at her, darting forward and viciously kicking her; rolling away, she gave a leap without making a sound, and disappeared.

Hagg Abd Rabbuh

When he was enveloped by the dark lane, he slowed his pace. The doors of the houses were still open, with a faint light seeping from them. She was behind him; he sensed this without turning round. He left the dark lane for the wide street. At that moment he turned and saw her coming, limping as she walked. When she saw him standing there, she stopped. People were coming and going in the street, talking and standing in front of the open shops; apart from them the street was almost empty. Their voices were lowered in the night. The two of them crossed the street. She was walking behind him, keeping the distance between them. Sometimes the strong light would draw her to one of the shops. She would stand for an instant gazing at the goods inside and would then quicken her pace.

He stood in front of the house. Turning, he saw her over there, hopping along in the empty open square.

His eldest daughter wakes him at dawn, carrying the bowl and ewer for him to make his ablutions. She keeps shaking him until he gets up. His body is tired. She has brought him his cloak and shawl. She follows him to close the door behind him. She brushes away with her hand the dirt that is clinging to the back of the cloak. The continuing slaps of her hand hurt him and he almost tells her off. The creaking of the door in the deep stillness.

He gave a slight cough as he crossed the threshold; his daughter behind him invoked the name of God. It seemed he was somewhat late, for the twilight of dawn that he was accustomed to had been replaced by the light of morning. He saw her on the stone platform of the neighboring house, stretched out on her side, pillowing her head on her arm. She sat up suddenly as though the noise of his leaving had woken her. When she saw him, she rushed off at a run. He stood quietly staring after her. The voice of his daughter, asking him what had happened, brought him back to his senses. Returning, he passed by her to his room.

Hagg Abd Rabbuh

❖

The sound of the women's trilling cries, of drums, and of singing. One of them was calling him from the partly open door. It was his son's wife, who had brought him his tray of breakfast and had seated herself on the threshold. He asked her about the trilling cries.

"What, Hagg? You mean to say you don't know?"

He was silent. No doubt they had already told him. He waited for her to speak. She said it was for the circumcision of her son Ahmad. She was angry at him for forgetting. His grandson. But which one?

On his way outside he passed by the courtyard. It was crowded with women, men, and children. He had hardly reached the door before he saw her gazing at him from amid the crowd. Retreating slowly, she left by the open door. He awoke to the sudden silence around him. They were all looking at him. No doubt he had given a shout. His face was still trembling. He turned and went back to his room.

❖

He had left the village behind him and was making for the neighboring settlement when he saw her. Her sudden appearance did not anger him. He was walking along the canal and she was on the other bank. When the channel became narrow, he approached the bank and sat down on a rock in the shade of a tree. She too approached the edge and stood there.

"Whose daughter are you, girl?"

"Yes, I know you want to kill me."

Exposed to the bright rays of the sun, she was shading her eyes with her hand as she looked at him. Her gallabia was dusty and tufts of straw were clinging to her hair.

"And what do you want?"

"And what do I want?"

"You want to marry me."

She laughed suddenly. She wheeled around, supporting her weight on her heel. Then she stood up.

Hagg Abd Rabbuh

"Marry you? What's this about marrying you, Hagg?"

She laughed again and jumped up to touch the branch of the tree. She never stays still for a single moment. She hops about on one foot in the middle of the road. She comes and goes, gripping her other foot behind her back. He rose to his feet and returned home.

❖

They had lit the lamp in the small passageway adjacent to his room, and he was conscious of them as they came back to lower its flame.

He had no appetite for the evening meal and went back to bed. Between wakefulness and sleep, he was leaning over the water-course under the shade of the sycamore tree, lifting up her body from the dingy waters. Her hair was wet and sticking to her cheeks and thin neck. The light of the sun was so brilliant it hurt his eyes. Baffled, he draws her up a little way. She responds to him. Her small breasts. Drops of water cling to her thick eyebrows. There is a slight down on her upper lip. Her eyes sparkle merrily. A faint sound comes from afar. He remains lying down, moist with sweat. The sound comes back like a rustling. He raised his head, leaning on his arm. She was sitting by the open door, her legs stretched out into the room. He moaned breathlessly and pushed his legs out of the covering. She got to her feet and disappeared. He rushed along behind her, stumbling in the darkened corridor, until he reached the courtyard, and he saw them there. They were silent and turned toward him. He was in his underclothes staring into their faces. He saw his eldest son advancing toward him. He wheeled round and went back to his room.

They stood round him. They put another cover on him. Many faces. All those people. She was standing behind them, raising herself on her toes in order to look at him. Her small thin face. He closed his eyes.

War Widows

He stood at his office window looking into the courtyard. These days toward the end of the month the women in black were crowding round the windows where payment was made. He disliked nothing so much as seeing the women in black. The courtyard looked as though a crowd of crows had descended on it, with their quick mincing steps and their little leaps toward the windows. As he left home of a morning he would say, "Payment begins today. I shan't go."

He would look for some place to spend the day, and would say to the driver, "Go to the Nile."

He would stay inside the car staring out of the window at the river. He knew, though, that in the end he would go to the office.

He had given instructions for the payment of pensions to be properly organized. Signs were written in large letters over the windows: "Names up to letter F shall have pensions paid on the first and second days. Names from F to S shall be paid on the third and fourth days, while the remainder shall be paid on the fifth and sixth days."

Even so he would find the courtyard crowded on the first day, would see them standing about in confusion at the windows. They would enter the offices in an attempt to persuade the clerk to put forward the day of payment. Then they would return to the courtyard, far from the queues, and when the crush in front of the windows had died down they would renew their attempts.

"What do you expect? They're women who've lost their husbands in the war."

War Widows

It was one of the expressions for which he was famous at the office, his hand falling limply to the desk and tiny shadows of sorrow showing on his smiling face. Always they would have a decisive effect and a sudden silence would reign as those who had started to protest fiddled with their papers then collected them up, as one of them mumbled, "Quite right, sir. Quite right."

One day he asked himself, "Why in black?"

He was sitting by the window watching them through a small gap in the drawn curtain. Their faces looked extremely pale—with the dry traces of make-up, the black kerchief round their heads, the black shoes and black stockings, and that listless, wan look. "Maybe they lead another life of which we know nothing, and when they come here they make themselves look as they think we would like to see them."

The matter perplexed him for a long time. They could easily change their clothes and remove their make-up. But that look in their eyes. Could that be put on the moment they entered the place? The office building with its high walls and the tall trees around it, the cool stillness, the guard at the gate, and that regular, constrained movement of people—all these gave it an isolated character, with its own special, mysterious smell.

Crossing the courtyard, he would pass by them without stopping and they would make way for him. Sometimes, before proceeding upstairs, he would turn and say, "What— are your problems never ended?"

It was as if he had granted them permission to approach him. They would rush forward and crowd round him. Those meaningless questions, their attempts to be friendly, the wisps of hair fixed in place under the black kerchief with black hair-grips. He would stare into their faces with a frown. Then he saw her. He was standing on the broad marble stairway and she was coming toward him, small as a child, with her skinny bosom, her faded black dress. She was asking him about something and he was surprised by her

War Widows

faint voice, by its calmness. She stood a pace away from him and when, as usual, he wanted to show himself unconcerned, she had suddenly clutched at him. He was alarmed. It was the first time he had stared into one of their faces from so close up. That loathing in her eyes, the twist of the mouth, the pallid whiteness of her face, the faint trace of hair above her lip and on her cheeks. He submitted to the way she was pushing him, and when the clerk tried to drag her away she clung to him, screaming and squirming like a terrified cat. Then, suddenly, she struck him with her fist.

❖

As it was an extremely hot day he had opened the windows, and he was standing to one side. It was still early and the soldiers were gathering up the debris and flattening the ground of the courtyard with rollers. The women were coming and gathering in the shade of the trees along the length of the wall. In a matter of moments the color black was obscuring the wall opposite; in shadow in the middle where the shade stretched out broadly, in sunlight at the two ends. They were standing motionless, black handbags dangling from their hands, staring out in one direction toward the closed windows from which payment was made. A little before nine the sound of chairs being dragged along by the cashiers was heard. He saw the women scattering across the courtyard, rushing to the windows. Then he saw her, the little woman. She was standing over there under a tree, a hair-pin gleaming on the black headcloth fixed under her chin.

She came each day that pensions were paid out. He was astonished to discover that she was in fact quite aware of the dates at the beginning of the next month when her pension was due. She would remain standing over there under the tree until the windows were closed and the women had departed. He would then see her crossing the courtyard to leave, an envelope held in her hand.

The file was on his desk. He had brought it himself from the archives: those narrow passageways in the basement like long, twisting alleys. He had stood looking around him in

War Widows

amazement, as though seeing them for the first time: all those files tied up in bundles and the heaped up shelves. On the side of every passageway was a small notice in yellow: "War Widows Year . . . ." Alongside the last passageway was the notice in green, "General." It was precisely arranged, he told himself. Not badly done. It had been his idea, and he had himself taken part in the design of the notices. He remembered that it was he who chose the colors yellow and green. He had pointed to the design, saying, "You'll find the file in an instant. Just determine the year and the first letter of the name. The real confusion arises in getting those killed one year muddled up with those killed another."

He became conscious of a faint whispering behind him. The clerks in the archives section were following him, alarmed at his presence. He was flipping through the file when one of them said that the woman's papers were now complete and that she had been informed of the date when the pension would be payable next month.

"The husband twenty-seven. Married four years. B.A. in Commerce. One daughter aged two. Land mine explosion during the course of duty."

There was a photograph of the husband fixed to the top corner of the file. Nothing else. He looked at the photograph again: a long face, thin mustache, small smile. He shut the file. Nothing. Like any other file.

He was pacing in the office, coming to a stop behind the three payment windows. What was he looking for? The pension had been accurately calculated and was being paid on time. He knew that. Well? He was staring out toward her from behind the curtains. She was still there in the shade of the tree. The courtyard was almost empty of women.

He sent someone to call her. When he saw her following the soldier, he felt all of a sudden at a loss. He told himself there was no reason for her to come and see him.

She sat on a chair beside the door. The long black stockings, the thin legs, and the envelope—which looked as if it was empty—tightly folded in her hand.

War Widows

He told her he had read the file, and he pointed to the file in front of him.

She was staring into his face.

He said he had learned from the persons concerned that they had informed her of the date when her pension would be paid as from the beginning of next month. There was thus no problem.

He waited for her to say something, but she remained silent. She was looking at the things on his desk. Her eyes came to rest for a moment on the file, then she suddenly got up and went out.

It was an exceedingly hot day.

"Go to the Nile," he told the driver.

He sat in the car looking at the waters of the Nile. People were coming and going. "Take me home," he said to the driver.

Sources

'The Wastelands' (al-Barārī), 'Wild Mulberries' (al-Tūt al-barrī), 'Drought' (al-Jafāf), 'Uncle Zeydan' (al-ᶜAmm Zaydān), 'That's How it Was' (Hādhā mā kān), and 'Meeting' (al-Liqā') are from *Hādhā mā kān* (1988).

'At the Roadside' (ᶜAlā jānib al-ṭarīq) is from *Aḥlām rijāl qiṣār al-ᶜumr* (1979).

'My Grandfather' (Jaddī), 'A Last Glass of Tea' (Kūb al-shāy al-akhīr), 'On the Brink' (al-Ḥāffa), 'The Hill' (al-Tall), 'A Weak Light Revealing Nothing' (Ḍaw' ḍaᶜīf lā yakshif shay'an), 'A Conversation at Night' (Ḥadīth bi-l-layl), 'The Prisoner' (al-Sajīn), and 'The Condemned Man' (Iᶜdām) are from *Ḍaw' ḍaᶜīf lā yakshif shay'an* (1993).

'The Bend of the River' (Munḥanā al-nahr), 'The Girl Washes' (al-Bint taghtasil), 'Death Has its Time' (Li-l-mawt waqt), 'The Floating Sack' (al-Shuwāl al-ᶜā'im), and 'War Widows' (al-Arāmil) are from *Munḥanā al-nahr* (1992).

'A Conversation from the Third Floor' (Ḥadīth min al-ṭābiq al-thālith) and 'Confrontation' (al-Taḥaddī) are from *Ḥadīth min al-ṭābiq al-thālith* (1970).

'The Trap' (al-Fakhkh) and 'Hagg Abd Rabbuh' (al-Ḥajj ᶜAbd Rabbuh) were translated from manuscript.

MOHAMED EL-BISATIE is author of six volumes of short stories and four novellas, all published in Arabic. Born and raised in the Nile Delta, the venue of the stories in *A Last Glass of Tea*, he now lives in Cairo.

DENYS JOHNSON-DAVIES has been described by Edward Said as "the leading Arabic-English translator of our time." He has published more than twenty volumes of short stories, novels, plays, and poetry translated from modern Arabic literature.